Rockin' Winter

SAMANTHA MICHAELS

I have so many people to thank!
First and foremost is my husband and our dog!
My besties, the amazing JJ Grice and Lala Montgomery. Your support and more importantly, your friendship keeps me going!
Ayana & Nick - Thank you so much for believing in me and fighting for me!
Thank you Alyssa for the awesome job proofreading!
The amazing Carter Cover Designs!! Thank you for always giving me the most gorgeous covers!!
And finally, to the readers! Thank you for all the support!!

Chapter One

Lexi

"Mmmm, I love laying naked in front of the fireplace," I say as I sigh contentedly, while I'm laying in Damien's arms, head resting on his chest. I used to dread the cold winter nights, but that's all changed. Now, I get to spend those nights having sex with the hottest man ever. In just ten short days, we'll be married, something I never thought would happen to me.

"After growing up and living most of my life in California, I never thought I would enjoy cold weather, but baby, you've shown me what I've been missing," Damien says.

"I can't wait for you to see your first snowfall here. Maggie loves playing in it."

"I bet Dave will too. I'm just glad we got that retractable closed patio, so we can still be outside with them."

"Me too." I yawn, completely spent after the amazing passion I just experienced.

"Let's go to bed, babe," Damien whispers. He gets up and puts his robe on, so he can let the dogs out.

I do the same and join him. When the dogs are done, we bring them in and lock up, then head upstairs and climb into our warm bed, still naked. Damien lays behind me, spooning me and the warmth of his skin against mine always feels amazing. I fall asleep to the sound of him snoring. Even his bear-like snores are sexy!

The last Saturday before Christmas arrives and we're having a karaoke celebration at the club before we close for the holidays. I want my staff to have plenty of time with their families, plus, we need to get things ready for our wedding, which we're having here. After a leisurely breakfast, we head down to the club to make sure everything's ready for tonight. When we're done, we run out for a few last-minute gifts and a couple of prizes for tonight, then head home to decorate our tree.

I will confess that I love this holiday and all its pretty decorations. The yard and the outside of the house are done. Damien just shook his head when he saw the vast amount of decorations I have. I can't resist the vintage blow molds and lights. I could give Clark W. Griswold a run for his money! The inside's done as well, so all that's left is our tree. As is my personal tradition, I put on National Lampoon's Christmas vacation while we decorate.

"This movie again," Damien sighs.

"What? This is only the fifth time. I'm way behind my record." I laugh.

Despite his protests, he's laughing just as loud as me. It really doesn't matter how many times I've seen it, I still laugh as if it's my first. Once we have all the decorations on the tree, all that's left is the angel. I take it out of the box and Damien shakes his head.

"Hey, I love Tweety Bird," I say.

"You are a Tweety bird," he teases as he reaches up and secures my Tweety-Angel on the top of the tree.

"Cute," I say. "Now that we're all decorated, I would love to unwrap something."

"No presents until Christmas morning," he warns.

I walk over and unfasten his jeans. "I didn't say anything about a present."

"Well, who am I to deny your wish?"

"Good. Now get that hot ass naked and on the couch," I command.

He sits down, then reaches next to the couch and puts a Santa hat on. "Come sit on Santa's lap and tell him what you want. I wanna see your name on the naughty list, woman!"

"Mmmm, I want you to stuff my stocking with your mammoth cream-filled candy cane."

"Cute, but I said I wanted naughty."

"Fine. You want naughty, you got naughty. But I'm going to show you, not tell you. Close your eyes."

I remove everything except my bra and panties. "Open your eyes, Santa," I say.

"Holy fuckin' shit, woman."

I stand in front of him wearing only candy cane striped underwear. I remove my bra. Starting at my naked boobs, I run my hands down my body and slowly slide my panties off. Damien just sits with his tongue hanging out. I walk over to the couch and stand between his legs. I take a couple of fingers and tease myself while he watches.

His chest rises as his breathing shallows. He just sits, staring as I finger myself. When I'm extra wet, I lower myself into his lap, taking him deep inside. I grab the Santa hat and put it on. We fuck hard and fast, quickly coming undone.

Laughing, I say, "So, did I make the right list?"

He gives me a light smack on my naked ass and says, "Mmmm, yes you did, baby."

We head upstairs to shower and get ready for tonight.

I'm treating the crew to a party bus so we can all ride together, including our animals. All the dogs and Mikael's cat will hang out in my office. Judd walks over and waits with us until the bus arrives. I can't help but wonder if he'll join in and sing tonight. As if he's reading my mind, he says, "Is it too late for me to get on the list for tonight?"

"No, we won't open the list until the night starts, and I plan on putting my VIP friends at the top if they want to sing," I answer.

"Thanks," he says. I swear I see a gleam in his eye. Does he have something special planned for Mel? I can't wait to find out. If it kills me, I'm going to get those two together. Once we've picked up the rest of our friends, the bus drives us to the club. I invite the driver to join us inside so he doesn't have to sit on the cold bus, which he gladly accepts.

He takes the dogs upstairs for us and then hangs out in the employee lounge. We all sit at the VIP table down front. I walk over to the bar and help Cassie carry pitchers of beer and glasses to our table. She also takes our food order.

I walk up on stage a little while later and kick off the Karaoke. I have Judd first up on the list, so I call him up to the stage. Mel's jaw drops and her eyes twinkle. I know that look anywhere, but she refuses to admit she has feelings for him. Judd shows me what song he wants, and I try not to react. I walk back to the table and seat myself so I can watch Mel's face.

Damien whispers in my ear, "Do I want to know what song?"

"Oh just you wait!" I answer.

Bad Company's "Feel Like Makin' Love" starts playing and Damien's jaw drops. I look up at Judd and see his gaze focused on Mel. I look over at her just as a dreamy look washes over her face. She locks eyes with Judd as he sings. They look like they are the only two people in the room. Hannah's next to me and leans over. "Are they together?" she whispers to me.

"Not yet, but they should be," I say.

Every time Judd gets to the chorus, he smiles at Mel and her face gets more dreamy. After the song ends, Judd rejoins the table. The rest of us just sit, mouths agape at what we just witnessed. I know my phone is going to be ringing off the hook tomorrow. Scott has the list, so he takes care of calling everyone else up when it's their turn, while Cassie runs the machine. A few patrons sing, then I hear Mel's name. She didn't tell me she was going to sing. I know she has an amazing voice, and I can't wait for everyone to hear it.

She walks up to the stage and shows Cassie what song she wants. I hear Eternal Flame by The Bangles start and my eyes fill with tears. Mel opens her mouth and I watch the table. Jaws drop when they hear her beautiful voice. She locks eyes with the cowboy, and I see that same dreamy look on her face. My heart swells when I see them, and I hope they can find their way to each other.

When the song ends, Mel walks off the stage. Instead of returning to the table, she runs off toward the restrooms. I immediately get up to go check on her. She's sitting on the floor, tears pouring down her face. Helping her up, I say quietly, "Come on, let's go up to my office."

We walk upstairs. I send Damien a quick text letting him know. Mel flops down on the couch. "What the hell did I just do?" she asks.

"You sang a beautiful song."

"Come on, Lex. You know what I mean."

"Talk to me. I'm your best friend."

"I think I'm falling for him. But I can't. I just can't."

"Give me one good reason why not."

"I'm damaged goods."

"I said a good reason. I love you and I hate seeing you like this."

"Please, Lex, I just can't."

"But- "

"No. My family's right. I'm meant to be alone."

Before I can say anything else, Mel goes back to the table. I follow her and sit down. Damien looks at me and I shake my head. He nods, knowing he'll get the story when we get home. The rest of the night is a blast. Once the event is over, I wish the staff well and tell those who are helping with the wedding to watch for group texts. I join Damien and our friends on the bus and we all head home.

We're the last ones dropped off, along with Judd. After spending the entire ride staring at his feet in silence, he says goodnight and heads home before we can ask him anything. We take the dogs out back to use the potty, then head inside. We're lying in bed when Damien asks me about Mel.

"This needs to stay between us," I say. "She has feelings for him, but she refuses to give in to them."

"I think it's the same for Judd. I just wish I knew what was holding them both back."

"I know Mel's and I'm determined to help her overcome it, but I don't know that we'll ever know about Judd."

"Maybe spending all the extra time together preparing for our wedding will spark things," Damien says.

"Mmm, I can't wait for that day. I love you."

"I love you more."

Chapter Two

Damien

"Babe, you almost ready," I call into the bedroom.

"Yeah, just finished wrapping Holly, Cocoa, and Leo's Christmas presents."

She comes downstairs in a Santa hat and Buddy the Elf sweater and I just shake my head. It really doesn't matter what she wears. She's the sexiest woman in any room. She puts the gifts into a bag, grabs the bottle of wine we bought for Dean and Alex, and puts that in the bag.

"Can you get me a couple more bags," she asks.

"For what?"

"Presents for everyone else."

"You're amazing. How did you find time to get all this done?"

"Elves," she teases.

I grab her two bags and watch as she packs up gifts for all of our friends. I help her carry the bags to the car. We come back and get food and treats packed for the dogs, leash them up and head over to Dean and Alex's house. The only ones who haven't yet arrived are Judd and Mel. All the women are in the kitchen with Alex. I hear them all asking Lexi about karaoke night. She doesn't say much but asks that they not mention anything once Judd and Mel get here.

Lexi grabs our bags and hands out the gifts she brought for everyone. She walks over to where all the dogs and Leo are laying and gives them their gifts. The sounds of squeaky dog and cat toys fill the room. When she's done, she comes and sits with me. Damn, she smells so sweet. I would never admit this out loud, but I love when she uses her vanilla-scented shower gel. If I could, I'd take her right here.

When Judd and Mel arrive, Lexi walks into the kitchen while Judd comes out to the living room. When dinner's ready, the women all help Alex carry the food to the table. Once we're all seated, Dean stands up. He raises his champagne flute and we all follow suit.

"In just one week, we'll all be together celebrating Alexis and Damien's wedding. Cheers to you both. Thank you so much to my beautiful wife for preparing this amazing meal. And thank you to all of you for joining us. We truly are a family."

We all clink glasses and dig into the food. Just like on Thanksgiving, I join the other men in cleaning up so our ladies can relax in the living room. When we're done, we join them and have our gift exchange. Wrapping paper is flying everywhere like we're a group of children waiting to see what Santa brought. I look at Lexi and my heart swells at the look of pure joy on her face.

We're all taking turns showing off our gifts and thanking each other. I love this family we've all become. Now, we just need to get our last two singles paired off. If only they could be our Christmas miracle. Dean grabs a trash bag and we pass it around, cleaning up all the paper. It's close to eleven when we all get ready to head home. We all hug goodbye and firm up plans for the rehearsal next week.

After we get home we put all the gifts under the tree, then take the dogs out for their last bathroom break. It's cold out, so I pull Lexi close to me. She nestles into me, making my heart swell again. We lock up and head to bed.

I wake before Lexi and just lay there, watching her sleep. A little while later, she stirs and opens her eyes. I pull her close and kiss her softly.

"Merry Christmas, baby," I say.

"Merry Christmas, my love," she says.

I pull her closer and kiss harder this time. She moans into my mouth as our tongues intertwine. We get up a few minutes later and grab a shower. After a quick breakfast, we head into the living room to give the dogs their presents. Lexi laughs as both dogs tear into the wrapping paper and play with their new toys. I've loved that sound since the first time I heard it.

Lexi and I agreed to one gift each for each other, though I have a secret second gift planned. I open mine first and can't believe my eyes. I'm staring at my band's debut album from back in the 80s, along with some promotional photos. Lexi arranged everything in a beautiful frame that will go perfectly in my music room.

"Babe, this is amazing. How did you find these?"

"I found everything on eBay."

"Thank you so much."

"My pleasure."

I hand a gift to her and keep my eyes locked on her face. She opens her box and tears fill her eyes as she sees the beautiful photo collage from the day we got engaged.

"Oh, Damien. This is the best present I've ever gotten. This day means so much to me, and I love seeing it captured like this."

"Mel captured some incredible shots."

"She absolutely did. I love this. Thank you!"

"You're welcome. Now I have one more present, but you have to go in the kitchen and keep your eyes closed."

"We agreed to one each!"

"I'm a rebel. Trust me, you're gonna love this one."

She smiles and walks into the kitchen. I wait until she closes her eyes and I get ready. When I'm ready, I call her back to the living room.

"Baby, come open your special present."

She saunters over with an extra shake in those sexy hips of hers. She takes the lid off of the box and a smile spreads across her beautiful face.

"Oh, Damien, just what I always wanted. Your dick in a box. And now, I want a taste."

She lowers her head. "You may want to remove the box first, babe."

"This is more fun."

I watch as she puts her face into the box. I feel her soft lips wrap around my already-hard cock. She runs her lips up and down my shaft a few times, then stops. Such a tease, my woman. Suddenly, she mumbles something, but with my dick in her mouth, I have no idea what.

"I could understand you better if your mouth wasn't around my dick."

"Stuck. Stuck. Stuck," she mumbles, sounding like Flick when his tongue stuck to the flagpole in A Christmas Story.

I laugh uncontrollably. "Is your head stuck in the box?"

"YES!" she mumble-shouts.

I have an idea, but I can't stop laughing. She puts her hands on her hips and clears her throat. The vibration drives my dick wild, but I need to focus on getting her head out of the box. I take a deep breath to compose myself.

"Lift your head straight up and walk backwards," I tell her.

Her mouth is finally off my dick, but she stumbles and ends up on her ass, the box still stuck on her head. I know I need to help her, but dammit, I need to do something first. I grab my phone and snap a picture of her, and I know I'm going to catch hell for that. But, to my surprise, she laughs hysterically. I get off the couch to help her. Instead of getting up, though, she pulls me to the floor with her and crushes her lips to mine.

She pushes me onto my back and wraps her sexy mouth around my dick to finish what she started. She bobs her head up and down, her tongue running along my shaft as she sucks me hard. Fuck, she's so damn good at that.

"Oh god, woman, I'm about to give you a treat."

"Mmmm," she moans, and the vibration sends me over the edge. She swallows every drop, then lies on her back and opens her legs for me. I slide my head between her sexy thighs and give her a tongue lashing like she's never had. She quickly comes undone, her body writhing on the floor. We head upstairs and grab a quick shower so Lexi can start dinner. Judd's joining us for dinner, and I'm glad he accepted Lexi's invitation. I'd hate to see him spending the holiday alone.

We get downstairs just as we hear a knock on the door. I answer it and I wish it surprised me who's standing there.

"Please come in," I say and walk her to the kitchen.

Chapter Three

Lexi

"Merry Christmas, Lex," I hear a familiar voice say.

"Merry Christmas, Mel," I answer as I turn around. "Oh no, I can tell by the look on your face it's not been a great day so far."

"No, it certainly has not. I was again uninvited to dinner as I refuse to change my stance on giving money to Trish."

"Sweetie, I'm so sorry."

She suddenly notices what I'm doing. "I shouldn't have come. I'm keeping you from getting dinner ready," she says, fighting back tears.

"Nonsense. You're my best friend and you're always welcome here. In fact, I'm going to insist that you stay for dinner. Judd's coming, so it will just be the four of us and the furries."

"I couldn't."

"Hush. Please go make yourself at home. Judd should be here in about an hour, so I want to get the food in the oven."

"Can I help? I would feel better if you let me."

"Okay, I have a job for you." I hand her a can of pineapple slices and some toothpicks. "I just need some pineapple on the outside of the ham."

"Aye, aye, captain," she teases.

Once Mel's done, I put the ham and the macaroni and cheese in the oven. I have a bowl of Coleslaw in the fridge and the only other thing I need to cook is the green beans, but I'll wait a while on those. Mel grabs a couple of treats for Maggie and Dave, then takes a seat on the couch. Damien's in the recliner and I'm about to squeeze in next to him when I hear the door. I answer the door and get a big hug from the hunky cowboy. Damien joins us and the guys shake hands.

Damien stays with me in the kitchen and we watch Judd walk into the living room. Mel stands up and Judd gives her a big hug. I watch her knees buckle, but she catches herself. Damien gives me a little squeeze on my hand as we watch them. They look perfect together. If only we could help eliminate the obstacles keeping them apart. They break the hug and sit down on the couch. They start talking, so Damien and I hang back in the kitchen. With our house's open floor plan, we can hear their conversation.

"How come you aren't with your family, if you don't mind me asking," Judd says.

"Issues with my sister," Mel says.

"Sorry to hear that. I understand family issues more than most," Judd says.

"It's tough. If you ever want someone to talk to, I'm a good listener," Mel says.

"Thank you, ma'am," Judd says.

I see Mel smile at him and he smiles back. Maybe we'll get our Christmas miracle after all. At the very least, it appears a friendship is forming. Dinner is close to being ready, so I get my Christmas-themed dishes out of the cabinet. Damien grabs them and sets the table for me. He grabs the fancy silverware and puts that out, then the glassware. He fills the water glasses and the wine glasses. Mel joins me in the kitchen to see if I need help. She has that dreamy look on her face again.

"You look happy, girl," I say.

"Don't start. It can't happen and you know why," Mel says.

"Come on, do you really think that would make a difference to him?"

"I can't take that chance. It would hurt too much."

I nod, wanting to say more, but not wanting to upset my friend. Turning my focus to getting the green beans in the pot I get some of the other food ready to serve. I grab the Coleslaw out of the fridge and put a spoon in the bowl. Mel carries that to the table while I get the ham and the macaroni and cheese out of the oven. Damien takes care of slicing the ham while I finish up.

Once all the food is on the table, Damien grabs his wine glass, gives a quick toast and we all clink glasses. I can't help but watch Mel and Judd interact as the food is being passed around. I've seen quite a few stolen glances and dreamy looks between them. It breaks my heart that they're both so resistant to pursuing this. But, they will be together quite a bit over the coming week as we get closer to the big day, so who knows?

After dinner, everyone helps me carry things to the kitchen. As is customary, I made too much food, so I pack up containers for Judd and Mel to take home and put the rest in containers for Damien and me to have leftovers. Once the kitchen is cleaned up, we all sit in the living room and chat for a bit. Most of the talk ends up being about the wedding and firming up plans.

A little after seven, Judd gets up. "Thank you both so much for dinner," he says to Damien and I. "I have a busy day tomorrow, so I'm going to head to bed early tonight."

I can't help wondering if Mel wishes she was going to bed with him, but I quickly push that naughty thought away. Damien walks to the closet to grab Judd's coat. Mel gets up too, and says, "I'm exhausted, so I think I'll head out as well." Damien hands both of them their coats. We all hug good night. Damien and I stand on the porch and watch Judd walk Mel to her car before heading over to his ranch.

"Brrr... it's cold," I say as Damien shuts the door.

"How about we make some hot chocolate and cuddle under a blanket? I have a little surprise for you," he says.

"You always know exactly what I need," I say.

"Mmmm, yes I do, woman."

Damien pulls out the sofa bed, and we get snuggled under a blanket.

He turns on our Amazon Firestick and pulls up a queue of movies he setup for me. I squeal when I see my four favorite Christmas movies: National Lampoon's Christmas Vacation, A Christmas Story, Elf, and, of course, Die Hard. Damien puts his arm around me and pulls me close. I lay my head on his shoulder as we sit and binge all four movies. By the time we're done, we're both so exhausted, we don't even have the energy to go upstairs. Damien puts the dogs out and locks up. We get back on the sofa bed and that's the last thing I remember until I'm awakened by two barking dogs.

I try to get out of bed, but Damien stops me. "Please stay in bed, baby."

"I can't. The final dress fitting is today, so I need to get ready."

Damien and I are in the kitchen eating breakfast when Mel arrives.

"Bring her back in one piece," he teases.

"She's safe with me," Mel says.

Mel finds a spot in front of the bridal shop and parks. We head inside and Helen's waiting for us. A few minutes later, the rest of the girls arrive. Helen brings out a rack with all the dresses on it. We go into the dressing rooms and change. Helen has me wait until the other girls are ready and out front.

"Okay, Lexi, you can come out," Helen says.

I walk out and tears pour down Mel's face. "Oh my god, you're stunning," she says.

The other girls agree.

"You're all stunning," Helen says. "Line up by height next to Lexi so I can get a picture."

Helen snaps a picture of each of us, then texts it to our phones. Helen checks all the dresses and they all fit perfectly. We all change, then she puts each dress back in its bag. We're going to keep them all locked in my office at the club since we'll be changing there. Alex arranged for the staff at our favorite hair salon to come there for hair and makeup. The men will get dressed at my house since I'll be staying at Mel's house the night before.

We all hug Helen goodbye, then head to our favorite pizza place, Palermo's, for lunch. Mel orders wine for everyone and stands, her glass in her hand. "To the most beautiful bride ever. I love you, Lexi. May you and that sexy rockstar have an incredible life together."

We all clink glasses and wait for our pizza to arrive. We're all talking and laughing as we eat. I swear I hear someone making pig noises, then it stops so I chalk it up to hearing things. A couple minutes later, I hear it again, but louder. Looking around the restaurant, my eyes land on the last two people I want to see.

"Lex, what's up?" Mel asks. She turns to see where I'm looking and her face turns red. "They better stay away from this damn table," Mel says. We don't get our wish and watch as my parents stand at our table.

"Well, well, well, it's the piggy and her little friends," my mother says.

I'm about to respond when Hannah stands up, her hands clenched into fists at her sides. "Who the fuck do you think you are? Your daughter is one of the sweetest, kindest, and most beautiful women I've ever known. You, on the other hand, are a disgusting piece of garbage. Now, I strongly suggest you get away from our table."

Palermo's owner approaches our table. "Ladies, are these people bothering you?" he asks, pointing at my parents.

"Yes. Could you please ask them to leave?" Hannah says.

He nods. "You're bothering my best customers and personal friends, so you'll need to leave and not return."

"Whatever, I'm tired of looking at her anyway," my mother says as she and my father head to the door.

Hannah sits down. "I'm so sorry. She just reminded me of my mom and I lost it," Hannah says.

"No need to apologize," I say. "Thank you for defending me."

"Us gals need to stick together," Hannah says.

When I get home, I fill Damien in on what happened. Being the incredible man he always is, he orders us Chinese food and queues up some of my favorite comedies. We stay up way too late watching them, but it was exactly what I needed.

Chapter Four

Damien

The next morning, we sleep late, then grab a quick shower and a bowl of Lexi's childhood favorite Froot Loops for breakfast before Scott and Cassie come over to make final plans for the music. I sit on the couch and Lexi sits in my lap. Pulling her close, I crush my lips to hers. My dick stirs as we kiss and I need to fight hard to talk it down, at least until after Scott and Cassie leave. A knock at the door interrupts our tonsil hockey game. Lexi slides off my lap and when I get up to answer the door, I feel a smack on my ass.

"What was that for?"

"For soaking my panties with that passionate kiss."

"I promise I'll make it up to you," I say with a wink.

She smiles and says, "Mmmm, I can't wait."

I open the door and walk Scott and Cassie to the living room. Lexi stands and hugs them both, then invites them to sit on the couch. I take the chair and, of course, little miss naughty takes my lap. I try to fill my head with things that will keep my dick from giving away how badly I want this woman.

"So, what are you thinking music-wise?" Scott asks.

"I'd like to go for a mix, stuff that's easy to dance to. Just none of those cheesy group dances," Lexi says.

"Thank you. I hate playing those, but when the client wants them, I go along with it," Scott says.

"Have you decided what you want for your first dance?" Cassie asks.

"Yes. We decided on an eighties hair metal classic, Firehouse's Love of a Lifetime," I answer.

"Oooh, good choice," Cassie says.

"Okay, I think I have everything I need," Scott says. "We'll see you on New Year's Eve."

Lexi gets up and hugs Cassie while Scott and I shake hands. I walk them to the door, then return to the living room. One look at Lexi and I know it's time for my dick to have some fun.

"Upstairs now. I have to get inside you," I command.

After tearing each other's clothes off, we jump into bed.

"Oh god, Damien, that was incredible," Lexi moans after we spend the afternoon fucking.

After waking up from a leisurely nap, we enjoy a sexy shower together then go downstairs to have dinner. Lexi makes me her favorite cool weather meal, a grilled cheese sandwich and a bowl of tomato soup. After we eat, we feed the dogs, then take them out for a walk around the neighborhood.

"Baby, I can't believe we're so close to the wedding," I say.

"Me either," she whispers.

"You don't sound too thrilled."

"I'm sorry. I'm excited, but scared at the same time."

"But, I love you."

"I love you. Trust me, it's not you."

"Talk to me, doll."

"I'm worried my parents will do something."

"They won't."

"You don't know that."

"Yeah, I do. I wasn't going to tell you this. I wanted to spare you. I asked the club's security to watch for them and not let them in. I found pictures on social media and sent them to the team."

"How is it you always know exactly what I need?"

"Because I'm the perfect man," I joke.

"You truly are," she says. "I love you so much."

We walk a little further in silence until the dogs decide to stop in Grumpy McDickhead's yard to do their business. He hates anyone even looking at his yard, let alone pets using it as a toilet. Lexi swears Dave and Maggie do it on purpose. She quickly cleans it up before he sees us and we scurry down the road.

"I think we need to let those two run in the yard a bit," Lexi says when we get back home.

"Me too. They're crazy." I laugh.

After we're in the backyard, we let the dogs off their leashes and watch them chase each other around the yard. Lexi laughs as she watches and damn if that sound doesn't do something to me every time I hear it. I stand behind her and wrap my arms around her. She looks over her shoulder at me, an amused look on her face.

"Um, is that a banana in your pocket?"

"Nothing in these pockets."

"You're such a horn-dog."

"Damn right when I'm around you, woman."

Lexi turns to face me and grinds against my growing erection. We call the dogs inside and make it as far as the living room couch before we're pawing at each other. After a quick fuck on the sofa, we head upstairs to get in our comfy pajamas. When we're back downstairs, we give the dogs a couple treats and watch as they snuggle together and quickly fall asleep. We grab some popcorn and Lexi's obsession, Cherry Pepsi Zero, then snuggle on the couch and watch her favorite romcom, My Big Fat Greek Wedding. I look over at her after the movie ends and tears are sliding down her cheeks.

"Hey, what's wrong, sweetie?"

"I'm sorry."

"Never a need to apologize. Tell me what's going on."

"It's just watching the wedding scene. The way Maria carries in Toula's dress and the way her aunts help her get ready."

I put my arm around her and she rests her head on my shoulder. "I can't imagine how hard it is the way your mom treats you."

"It is, but I promise I won't let it darken our day. I've never been more excited about anything."

Lexi grabs a tissue and cleans her face, then we put on the Greek Wedding 2 before heading off to bed.

Time seems to fly as we get closer to the wedding. We're down to three days now. After another fun day of passionate sex, I ask Lexi what she wants for dinner.

"I could go for something Italian."

"Spaghetti and meatballs sound good?"

"Mmmm, yum. And for dessert, some cannoli."

"We don't have any."

"You do," she says as she points toward my crotch. I smile and shake my head. Turning my attention to dinner, I walk to the fridge to get a container of homemade sauce out. I put it in a pot and turn the burner on. The split second I move to the cabinet to get the pasta out, a pair of hands squeeze my ass.

"Good lord," I say.

"I can't help it. Men look so sexy when they cook. Gordon Ramsey's my secret fantasy lover."

"Ah, so you like 'em bossy, huh?"

"Oh, yeah!"

Well, she better get ready for later. We're gonna have some fun.

"Wanna help me, baby?"

"Of course. Awaiting my instructions, chef."

"Get the garlic bread ready."

"You got it."

I turn the oven on to warm up the bread and Lexi puts it in once she's done. I have the meal under control, so she sets the table, then gets dinner for Maggie and Dave.

"Baby, you're the hottest sous chef ever," I say.

"Mmm, I love cooking with you," Lexi says, a naughty smile on her face.

"I can't wait until you taste my cannoli," I say. Lexi giggles and my dick twitches.

We both grab our wine glasses and lift them. "A toast to the most beautiful woman in the world. I can't wait until you're my wife."

"To us," she replies. We clink glasses and each take a sip. Lexi fills her plate and moans after taking a bite. Hearing her soft moan and watching her enjoy my food turns me on, and my dick threatens to give me away. Down, boy, I think to myself, at least until later! She finishes her plate with no problem. I'm glad she's not one of those women who won't eat in front of a man.

"Wow, that was delicious," she says. "You have a real talent for this. Ever thought of cooking professionally?"

"Funny you say that. It was always something I thought about but never pursued."

"Well, maybe we could expand the menu at the club."

"Hmmm. Something we can talk through after we get back from our honeymoon."

"Yeah. Speaking of honeymoon, when do I get to find out where we're going?"

"Not until they call our flight."

"Damn! The wait is killing me!"

"It'll be worth it."

She smiles at me, and my heart skips a beat. I still wonder sometimes how I got so lucky to find her. Even more, I wonder how other men missed how incredible she is. Clearly, they had their heads shoved too far up their asses. We put the leftover food in containers, then get the kitchen cleaned up.

"I need to walk off some of that yummy food," she says as she grabs the dogs' leashes.

I smile, knowing she'll get one hell of a workout later. "Sounds good. Let's go. Wanna place a bet on whether the dogs do their business in Grumpy's yard?"

"You're on," she says, laughing. "What are the terms?"

"Whoever wins gets to make the other act out a naughty fantasy."

"So really, there's no loser then!"

"I bet they won't," I say.

"And I think they will."

We get the dogs ready and head out. As we walk, the dogs sniff every yard. "Come on, doggies, do your business," I say at each yard.

"Hey, St. James, that's cheating."

"We didn't set any rules, woman."

"Oh, I see. That's how we're doin' this."

Lexi walks at her normal pace until we reach McDickhead's yard. She stops and just stands there while Maggie and Dave sniff.

"I don't think they want to go here," I say.

She ignores me and doesn't move. After another ten minutes, the dogs finally settle on a spot and both of them go into Grumpy's front yard.

"Ha," she yells, sticking her tongue out at me. She hands me the leashes so she can clean up, then we finish the walk home. Lexi struts the whole way. I feign annoyance, but secretly I can't wait to hear what her fantasy is. I'll do just about anything as long as it ends with me fucking her.

"So, baby, let's hear it. What's your fantasy?"

"Well, since we both kinda cheated, I'm only going to tell you part of it. You get to decide the rest."

"Sounds fair."

"I want you to pick a costume that matches something I love and wear it for me. I promise, if you do, you will get lucky!"

"And it can be anything?"

"Yeah."

"Okay."

As I'm thinking about what I want to get, I look around the house for ideas. Feeling hungry, I walk into the kitchen to grab a snack and when I open the cabinets, inspiration hits. And now, I have a mission tomorrow. I could give Lexi one hundred guesses and she won't figure this one out. Lexi grabs herself something to eat, then we snuggle up on the couch and put the TV on.

"Are we becoming a boring old couple?" I ask her.

"Truth, I've been thinking that a bit, too. I mean, not with sex, but like this."

"Well, how about we change that?"

"What're you thinkin'?"

"How about a bar where we can just be patrons?"

"That sounds perfect. And you know, bars are always a good place for some naughty bathroom fun!"

"I like the way you think, woman!"
****

The next morning after breakfast, I head out in search of my costume and after a few tries, find what I'm looking for. I can't help but laugh, trying to picture Lexi's face when she sees me. When I get back home, there's a note from Lexi that she ran down to the club to check on things for the wedding. Grabbing my bag, I head upstairs to shower and get the costume on.

The dogs look up when I come downstairs and greet me with head tilts. If that's how they react, I can only imagine what Lexi's going to say! Sitting on the couch is difficult, but I manage. Maggie and Dave won't come near me, instead just staring at me. I can't help but laugh at the looks on their faces. I stand and take a selfie so I can add it to a special wedding present I'm putting together, then sit back down and wait. When I hear her car pull into the driveway, I get up and stand just inside the front door. The door opens and Lexi stops dead in her tracks.

Chapter Five

Lexi

"Damien St. James, what in the ever lovin' hell are you wearing?"

"You told me I could pick a costume related to something you love. So, I chose Froot Loops. Figured maybe you had a crush on Sam."

"I think my favorite part is the top, especially the blue wings and the toucan head on top of your head," she says.

"I'm kinda partial to the bright orange legs and the tail feathers myself," I say, shaking my ass for her.

"You, my love, are a Froot Loop Dingus, to quote one of my favorite lines ever from Big Brother."

I grab my phone and snap a few pictures of my crazy man. You never know when they might come in handy!

"So, what'cha wearing under that thing?"

"Wouldn't you like to know?"

I walk toward him. "Yes, I would."

"Gotta catch me first." He takes off, flapping the costume's wings and screeching. I chase him, but even in that ridiculous outfit, he's too fast. We do several laps around the couch. Damien changes direction and grabs me, scooping me up into his arms. He carries me up to our bedroom and sits me down on the bed.

Damien grabs his cell and the next thing I hear is The Ramones' cover of Surfin' Bird. "Get ready, baby."

As I sit and watch him do his best Peter Griffin impression, I'm amused and oddly turned on at the same time. Unable to control myself, I let out the loudest snort ever. I sit on the bed, clutching my stomach and barely able to breathe. Damien turns around and shakes his tail feathers at me. My face aches and I rub my cheeks. The song ends, so Damien starts it again and walks over to me.

"This time, you're dancing with me! Get that sexy butt up!"

I imitate his moves, both of us laughing our asses off as we look like dorks. Damien pulls me into his arms, or should I say, wings, and kisses me. The costume's beak tickles my forehead and I can't help but laugh into his mouth as we kiss. He scoops me up again and pretends to fly me over to the bed. He drops me on my butt in the middle of the bed, then treats me to my first cereal mascot striptease.

I watch as removes the top part of the costume, revealing his naked chest. Looking down, I lose it again.

"What's so funny, babe?"

"Ummm... you're standing there in bird legs and umm..." I point down at his crotch. "Nice pecker," I tease.

He slides the rest of the costume off, giving me a full view of his erection. It doesn't matter how many times I see it, his dick still turns me on big time. I sit up and wag my finger. He stands in front of me, so I lean forward and wrap my lips around his inviting cock. Reaching around, I plant my hands on his ass as I slide my lips up and down his dick.

"Fuck, your mouth feels so good," he growls. Squeezing his ass hard, I suck faster, loving the taste of him. I swirl my tongue around his head, licking the pre-cum off. Taking one hand off of his ass, I tease his balls while I suck. His balls tighten as he gets ready for his release. I moan when I feel his dick empty down my throat. Lapping up every delicious drop, I look up at him and lick my lips.

"I guess you liked the costume," he teases.

"Oh yeah. But now, I want you to get me naked and fuck me."

"Damn! But first, I'm craving a taste of that sweet pussy."

He slides his hands under my shirt and lifts it off. My bra follows, and he clamps his mouth on my naked breasts. He gently pushes me onto my back and tugs at my jeans. I lift my ass so he can finish stripping me. I open my legs for him and he growls again. He just stands there, looking at me. For someone who was so afraid of what she looked like, I now get turned on when he watches me.

He buries his head between my legs and licks me hard and fast. Grinding against his face, I explode as my body quakes. He slides his body on top of mine and jams his tongue into my mouth. Tasting myself on his tongue, I moan. I feel him enter me, his dick sliding easily into my soaking wet folds. I wrap my legs around him, pulling him tight against me as he pounds me with thrusts that make my body lift off the bed. He lifts my ass off the bed, angling me so he can get deeper.

His dick hits my g-spot with each thrust and my body convulses in response. I cry out, seeing colors as I soak his dick, coming harder than ever before. After unleashing a long string of dirty words, including some new ones I just made up, my body tingles as I come down off of my sexual high. He shoots his second load, this time deep inside my pussy. He collapses next to me. I lay my head on his chest, listening to his heart race, both of us drenched in sweat and a few other fluids.

We grab a shower, then get dressed for our night out. I'm looking forward to just being a paying customer. After feeding the dogs, we let them play in the backyard for a while. Damien calls them in when we get hungry. I grab our coats and we head out. The bar is about half an hour away, so I'm starving by the time we arrive.

Damien spots two empty seats at the end of the bar, so we sit down. The bartender approaches, handing us each a menu.

"What can I get you folks?"

"Beer for me," Damien answers.

"Can I get a strawberry daiquiri?" I ask.

"Coming right up, then I'll take your food order."

He hands us our drinks, then grabs his notepad. Damien orders a burger and fries for each of us. Pointing at the board hanging behind the bar, I say, "Looks like we came on a good night. I love watching karaoke."

A little while later, our food comes. We also order another drink each. While we're enjoying dinner, the bartender walks over to the small stage and grabs the microphone. "It's karaoke time. Who's excited?" The other patrons cheer as he continues. "First up, we have a special treat for you tonight. Welcome fan favorites Judd and Mel to the stage."

I swallow the bite of burger I was chewing and look at Damien, my mouth hanging open. Damien's sporting the same look. We turn our stools to face the stage and, sure enough, we see our best friends walk out and stand in front of the microphone. The music to Peter Cetera and Amy Grant's duet, The Next Time I Fall, plays. When I hear them sing, looking at each other the entire time, my eyes fill with tears. Damien covers my hand with his as we watch the performance. The crowd goes wild for them. I can't help but wonder how long they've been coming here.

After a few more performances, the music comes back on and patrons fill the dance floor. As we finish eating, we see Judd and Mel in each other's arms, dancing. Judd leans toward Mel, looking like he's about to kiss her. Suddenly, he looks our way and spots us, so he pulls back. He tilts his head our way and Mel turns bright red when she looks over.

"How about we hit the dance floor and go talk to them?" Damien asks.

"Sounds like a plan."

I turn back around and Mel and Judd are nowhere to be found. We still dance for a few songs before we head out, but I sure am going to get answers tomorrow. Tomorrow night's our rehearsal dinner and I can't wait until Damien sees his surprise.

Chapter Six

Damien

I can't believe it's the day before I marry the most incredible woman. Lexi seems calm as she gets breakfast ready. We sit down to eat and I find out she's anything but.

"I'm never going to be ready for tonight," she sighs.

"What do you mean??" I ask.

"I look like a hot mess, I feel like a hot mess, I am a damn hot mess."

"I think you look gorgeous."

"Well, you need your damn eyes checked then," she snaps.

I walk over to her chair and kneel. Taking her face into my hands and gazing into her eyes, I say, "I promise you I've never seen a more beautiful woman than you. I love you."

"Oh Damien, I love you. Thanks for putting up with me."

"I'll put up with you as long as you keep playing with my dick," I tease.

That earns me one of her sexy little snort-laughs. Mission accomplished. Now I just need to figure out how to keep her calm. Turns out that was easier said than done. The day was filled with mini freak-outs until it was time for us to get ready for the rehearsal. We took a long shower together, and that helped her relax. Mel comes over to do her hair and makeup, and I can hear their conversation from the bathroom.

"Why did you disappear last night?" Lexi asks.

"What do you mean?" Mel asks.

"At the bar. We saw you and Judd, but when we hit the dance floor, you were gone."

"I didn't see you there."

"Judd was about to kiss you, then he saw us. You looked over, so I know you saw Damien and me."

"You need to lay off the romance novels. There's nothing going on between me and the cowboy. Whatever you thought you saw was all in your head. I'll wait for you downstairs."

I walk back to the bedroom and Lexi's just sitting on the bed. Joining her, I put an arm around her and say, "I know it's hard, but you just need to let this go. If they want to tell us anything, they will."

"I know, but I just want her to be happy."

"And that's one of many reasons I love you."

She smiles and my insides melt. Holding hands, we head to the restaurant for the rehearsal and dinner. I love seeing all our friends there waiting for us, though I feel a tug of sadness that Billy couldn't make it to the wedding. I love seeing all our friends there waiting for us, though I feel a tug of sadness that Billy couldn't make it to the wedding.

Once Judge Mathis, our officiant, arrives, the ladies leave the room to get ready for their processional while we guys line up. The doors open and one by one, Alex, Eden, Lizzie, and Hannah enter. Mel's next and I see Judd's face light up when she walks in. I still haven't caught a glimpse of my bride. Once all the ladies line up, the wedding march plays and I see Lexi appear at the door. My jaw drops when I see she's not alone.

"Did you know about this?" I ask Judd.

"We all did. It was Billy's idea to surprise you. Dean picked him up from the airport yesterday," Judd says.

After the rehearsal, Billy greets me with a big hug. "I wanted to surprise ya, so I called Lexi a few weeks back and set this up."

"I was so bummed you couldn't make it. This is great!"

The waitress assigned to our group stops by to take drink orders, so we all take our seats. After the drinks are served, our meals arrive. Lexi and I decided to give everyone a sampler plate of the entrée choices from the wedding. After dinner, we have about an hour of dancing. Then Lexi and I ask everyone to take their seats. We present the gifts to our bridesmaids and groomsmen. We wrap things up shortly after the gifts. The ladies are all staying at Mel's tonight, so I head home alone.

I pull into the driveway and see headlights following me in. Turning around, I see all the guys are here. I smile when I see Billy with them. "What're you all doing here?" I ask.

"Bros night. It was Judd's idea," Dean says.

"But don't think for one second we're helping you get ready in the morning," Mikael jokes.

We head inside and down to the basement. Mikael grabs the remote and puts the Flyers game on.

"Anyone up for a pool tournament?" Johnny asks.

Everyone agrees, so I throw everyone's name in a hat to pick the first two players. The winner of each game picks the next opponent, and the loser is out until one man's left standing. Andy and Mikael are up first. I grab the rack for nine-ball and get the table set for them. They play rock-paper-scissors for the break. Andy sticks his tongue out and gives Mikael the finger, as he pockets three balls on his break and looks like he has clear shots on the rest. One by one, Andy sinks his balls until only the nine-ball's left. He calls his pocket and makes the shot easily. Mikael never even gets a chance to play, but he's out.

"I'll challenge Judd," Andy says.

Judd breaks and clears the table. One by one, he picks the rest of us off and we declare him the winner. First poker, now billiards. What is he hiding? He sure seems to have lived a different life. I can't help but wonder if that past is what's keeping him from admitting his feelings for Mel.

"Earth to the future Mr. Lexi," Dean teases, snapping me out of my reverie.

"Ha, ha, dickhead," I say. "Just thinking about tomorrow. I want everything to be perfect for Lexi. She's worried that her parents might try something."

"We're not gonna let that happen," Dean says.

"I've given their photo to security at the club so they can watch for them. My baby is going to have an amazing day."

"You both will," Judd adds.

"Thanks, guys. We better call it a night. Lexi will kill me if I oversleep."

These guys are the closest thing I'll ever have to brothers, and I know how lucky that makes me.

"I'm gonna crash here, if that's cool," Billy says.

"Of course," I say.

After everyone else is gone, I grab two beers. Handing one to Billy, we sit at the kitchen table. "Man, I can't thank you enough for being here," I say.

"I wouldn't miss it. Jack talked so much about wanting to see you find the one. He truly thought of you like a son," Billy says.

"And we both know he was more of a father than my sperm donor."

"He'll be watching over us tomorrow."

"I know he will."

"Hey, I also wanted to say how touched I was when Lexi asked me if I would walk her down the aisle."

"She's amazing. I'll never understand the way her parents treat her."

"Some people are just assholes, sadly."

I yawn as I take the last sip of my beer.

"I need to get some sleep. Are you all set?" I ask.

"I am. Night, Damien."

"Night, Billy."

Chapter Seven

Lexi

I open my eyes the morning of the wedding and see a bunch of women sitting in chairs surrounding the bed in Mel's guest room. "The bride is awake," Helen shouts, reminding me of my favorite rom-com.

"Outta bed, missy, and get your cute butt in that shower," Mel jokes.

"Yes, ma'am," I say with a salute.

"Breakfast will be ready when you're done," Eden says.

Everyone but Mel heads to the kitchen. She walks over to me and tears stream down her face. "What's going on, sweetie?"

"I'm just so damn happy for you."

"I love you."

"Never forget, you were mine first."

"Nobody could ever replace my bestie!"

Mel gives me an enormous hug then joins the others in the kitchen. I get in the shower, and all I can think about is Damien. It was tough not sleeping with him last night, but I believe we'll more than make up for it tonight, though I don't expect we'll get much sleep!

I finish up in the shower and blow dry my hair. I throw on sweats, a t-shirt and sneakers then head to the kitchen. The delicious aroma of bacon and waffles fills my nose and my stomach rumbles.

"Your chair, m'lady," Hannah says with a curtsy.

Smiling, I see a chair decorated with tulle and balloons in the shape of wedding bells. These ladies are the best. I especially love that Helen's with us. She's been more of a mom to me in the short time I've known her than the woman who gave birth to me. Mel grabs a pitcher and a tray of champagne flutes and pours us each a drink.

"Mimosas in honor of our beautiful bride," Mel says, her voice cracking.

"To Lexi," the group says in unison. The room fills with the sound of glasses clinking. We all laugh and talk as we eat the delicious breakfast Eden cooked. I try to help cleanup, but they won't let me. After we're done, we all head to the living room and talk. A little while later, Alex's phone chirps.

"Our ride's here," Alex says.

My eyes go wide when I see the hot pink limo sitting in Mel's driveway. "Don't worry, it will be a proper white limo that drives you to the reception, but I couldn't resist the pink for this morning," Alex says.

"I love it," I say. The driver walks to the back door and helps each of us in. We each enjoy a glass of champagne as we ride to the club. Cassie greets us and takes us upstairs where the hair and makeup team is waiting. Roxy is on hair and Lacey is on makeup.

"Can someone grab the veil?" Roxy asks.

Helen hands her the veil and Roxy places it on my head. "I want to put your hair in an updo and curl it inside the veil. What do you think?" Roxy asks.

"I love that idea," I respond.

Roxy puts the veil aside and gets to work on the updo. The girls are all standing around just watching and talking loudly.

"What's with you all this morning?" I ask.

"We're your Greek cousins," Mel says.

"Excuse me, but what?" I ask.

"A certain sexy rockstar called and told me about the other night when you were watching Greek Wedding," Mel says.

"And I'm your Maria," Helen adds.

"Oh my god, I love you all so much," I say. "Please don't make me cry."

"Don't worry, I can work magic with my makeup," Lacey says and we all laugh.

The door to my office opens and Scott walks in with a Polaroid camera. "Fresh baklava," he yells out and snaps a picture of me. That elicits even more laughter.

"Perfect," Cassie says. "Now get the hell out of here. Women only," she teases.

Roxy finishes my hair and shows me. Inside the veil's headpiece, she has my hair in a pile of curls. I love the way it looks and feel my eyes tear up for the thousandth time today.

"I love it. Thank you," I choke out.

While Roxy gets to work on the other girls, Lacey grabs a washcloth and wipes my face. After she dries it, she gets started on my makeup. After everyone's makeup is done, we have about a half hour until the ceremony begins. Mel whispers something to Helen. She walks into my office and returns a minute later, carrying my wedding gown just like Maria in Greek Wedding.

We all pile into my office so the girls can help me into my dress, then get dressed themselves. When we're all ready, Helen goes downstairs and sets up a divider so we can come downstairs without being seen. She hands each of us our bouquet and sends each of my bridesmaids down the aisle one at a time. Billy stands with me, waiting for our turn. I peek at Judd when Mel starts her walk. His face lights up and a smile appears.

"It's time. You look stunning. Remember to keep your eyes on Damien. You want to see his reaction," Helen says. She quietly takes her seat as the wedding march plays.

"You ready?" Billy asks.

"I've been ready," I smile.

He leads me around the divider, as my eyes land on Damien's handsome face. His jaw drops when he sees me, an image that will forever live in my memory. Billy and I reach the front and stand next to Damien.

"Who gives this woman to be married?" Judge Mathis asks.

"I do," Billy says.

He places my hand in Damien's then takes a seat in the front row.

"We're gathered here today to join Damien and Alexis in the bonds of marriage," Judge Mathis begins. "If anyone has reason these two should not be married, speak now or forever hold your peace."

Silence.

"Very well. Damien and Alexis have written special vows to each other. Alexis, please share your vows with Damien."

"From the time I was a little girl, I dreamed of a moment like this, but never truly thought it would happen. My parents raised me to believe I would never be worthy of a man's love. Then, one crazy spring afternoon, I got knocked on my butt by a crazy dog. Thank you, Dave, for bringing me and Damien together. Damien, I love you more than words could ever say, and I plan on spending the rest of my days showing you what words can't."

"Damien, please share your vows with Alexis."

"The music business filled my life with success, fun, and money. But, something was always missing. Love. And then, I left LA and moved here, seeking a more peaceful life and hopefully, a woman to share that life with. I was giving up that hope and that's when my crazy dog intervened. Now, I have the pleasure of waking up every morning next to the kindest, most loving, and by far, most beautiful woman I've ever known. Lexi, I love you and I will cherish and protect you always."

"Damien and Alexis, please join hands."

I turn to Mel and hand her my bouquet then grab Damien's outstretched hands.

"Damien, do you take this woman to be your lawful wedded wife?"

"Damn right, I do."

"Alexis, do you take this man to be your lawful wedded husband?"

"I do."

"The rings please." Judd hands the rings to Judge Mathis.

"Damien, place this ring on Alexis's finger and repeat after me. With this ring, I thee wed."

I watch a beautiful gold band slide down my finger. "With this ring, I thee wed."

"Alexis, place this ring on Damien's finger and repeat after me. With this ring, I thee wed."

I tremble as I slide Damien's ring on him. "With this ring, I thee wed."

"By the power vested in me by the state of Pennsylvania, I now pronounce you husband and wife. You may kiss your bride."

Damien grabs me and lays a kiss on me that rivals those in the dirty romance novels I love reading. I turn to Mel and take my bouquet.

"Guests, it gives me great pleasure to announce for the first time in public, Mr. and Mrs. St. James." Applause and cheers fill my ears as Damien and I walk down the aisle, followed by our gorgeous wedding party.

Chapter Eight

Damien

"B ut, I'm starving," I complain.

"Just a few more pictures, please," Lexi begs.

"Jeez, we've been married less than an hour, and already, you're ordering me around," I tease.

"Keep it up, Mr. St. James, and no naked time tonight," she teases.

"I suggest you think that through, Mrs. St. James," I tease.

Hearing a sniffle, I look over to see Mel wiping her eyes again. "I can't believe my best friend is married. No one deserves happiness more than you," Mel says to Lexi.

"Except you," Lexi says as she hugs her friend. If only Judd and Mel weren't so stubborn, maybe they'd be together. I turn my focus back to the gorgeous woman in the wedding dress keeping me from food. The photographer takes the rest of the photos, then we can finally go eat. We get to the reception area and we're met by Helen holding a tray of hors d'oeuvres.

"You're a vision," I say to Helen as I grab a mini-quiche off the tray.

"One thing I have experience with is weddings," Helen replies.

"I'm so grateful. Especially for what you did for Lexi," I say.

"The dress is beautiful."

"I don't mean the dress," I say.

"She's a sweetheart. I'm so sorry she had to deal with such horrible parents," Helen says.

"Me too," I say.

Cassie comes out to let us know Scott is ready to introduce us, so we line up. I hear Rock and Roll All Nite by KISS play as Scott announces each couple. "Andy and Lizzie York. Hannah and Mikael Alfredsson. Johnny and Eden Davidson. Dean and Alex Fox. Now, we have our best man and best woman, Judd Walker and Melissa McNeill."

Lexi and I peek in and see our friends lined up, waiting for us.

"And now," Scott announces, "we have our guests of honor, Damien and Alexis St. James." I scoop Lexi up in my arms and carry her across the dance floor, to the cheers of all of our guests. "Now, let's watch our couple in their first dance as husband and wife."

Firehouse's Love of a Lifetime plays and I pull my bride into my arms. She looks up at me, her eyes teary, a huge smile on her beautiful face. I hold her tight against me as we sway to the music. Lexi waves the rest of the wedding party to join us. I turn her so she can see Judd and Mel. They're gazing at each other, as if nobody else is in the room. I wonder if they're already together. Apparently reading my mind, Lexi whispers, "I'd swear they were already a couple."

I nod before I crush my lips to hers. I can't wait to get her home tonight. The song ends and we take our seats at the head table. The wait staff serves the meals. After dinner, Scott invites everyone to the dance floor. About an hour in, we cut the cake. I restrained myself and didn't smash any on my new wife's face. She was not so nice and left me with a face full of icing. The party keeps going until the wee hours of the morning. By the time the limo dropped us off, we were both yawning. I unlock the door and open it.

I lift Lexi into my arms and say, "Welcome home, Mrs. St. James."

"Thank you, Mr. St. James."

I carry her inside and put her down in the kitchen. All I can think about is getting her out of that dress and into bed.

"So, how does it feel, baby?"

"How does what feel?" she teases.

"You're lucky you're so stunning, woman!"

"Seriously, it feels amazing. I truly never thought this would be me, but here I am! Now, please help me out of this dress. I feel like a snow beast," she laughs. "And, thank you, Mel told me the whole movie re-enactment was your idea."

"My pleasure. Speaking of which, I've been waiting all night to pleasure my wife."

"Mmmm, please, my sexy husband."

I watch Lexi's dress trail behind her as she heads upstairs. As I follow her, I wipe the drool off my mouth. I stand behind her and unzip her dress, lightly dragging my fingers down her skin as I do. I slide the dress off of her shoulders and it falls at her feet. She steps out of the dress, picks it up, and lays it on the chair. Lexi looks like an angel in her white lace bra and panties, but I know better. She removes the veil and lays it with the dress. We finish getting naked and climb into bed.

We're both so exhausted that we fall asleep before anything even happens. The next morning, we wake to the sound of my cell phone alarm. "Baby, we need to get up so we don't miss our flight," I say as I gently shake Lexi awake. She stretches and sits up, her eyes droopy. Damn, if she doesn't look even more beautiful like this!

"Hawaii, baby!" she exclaims, and her sleepiness disappears. We quickly shower and dress. While I take the luggage downstairs, Lexi gets Maggie and Dave's stuff together.

"I'm going to run them over to Judd's while you wait for the limo," I say.

"Okay."

I load the dogs and their stuff in my car and drive over to Judd's. He answers the door after a couple of knocks. "Rough night?" I ask, noticing his bed-head. A grin appears on his face for a split-second before disappearing just as quickly. I want more than anything to grill him, but I don't want to upset him.

"Thank you for taking care of the furries," I say.

"Anytime. Have a great time. I'll see you in two weeks," Judd says.

I wave as I head back to my car. The limo pulls into the driveway just as I'm parking in the garage. The driver follows me inside and grabs our luggage. We climb into the backseat while he places our bags in the trunk. A couple of hours later, he drops us off at Southwest's section of Philly International. We're flying first class, so we board first. About a half day after we take off from freezing cold Pennsylvania, we land in the tropical paradise that is Maui.

We head home two weeks later, having seen very little other than the inside of our beach rental. Anyone who says marriage is the kiss of death for your sex life never met Lexi. Marriage turned her into a turbo sex machine and I lost count of how many times we fucked. I think my favorite moment was her standing on the bed, shouting, "I'm Fuckzilla, hear me moan!"

We spend the rest of January working on the Super Bowl party we're planning to hold at the club. I work on the menu with the kitchen staff while Lexi handles the decorating with Cassie's help. It's late by the time we get home each night, but damn if that horn-dog I married doesn't still want sex every night! Not that I'm complaining.

Chapter Nine

Lexi

The opening riff of AC/DC's Back in Black wakes me out of a dead sleep.

"Hello."

"Lex, it's Mel."

"It's 2 AM. What the hell?"

"I need a ride and five hundred bucks."

"Where are you?"

"Lancaster police department."

"What the hell happened?" Damien stirs when he hears me.

"What's up, babe?" he mumbles.

I hold up my index finger and he nods.

"Please, just come get me and I'll explain on the way home," Mel begs.

"Okay, on my way," I say. She disconnects.

"Where're you goin' at this hour?" Damien asks.

"Lancaster PD. Mel got arrested. As I get out of bed, I say, "I need to go bail her out."

"I'm coming with you," Damien says.

"I'm fine. Stay with the dogs."

Damien reluctantly agrees as I throw on jeans, a t-shirt, baseball cap, and sneakers. I grab my coat and purse when I get downstairs, grateful that we have a heated garage. I make the short drive to the police station and head inside.

"May I help you?" the desk officer says. I read his name tag.

"Yes, Officer Nolan. I'm here for Melissa McNeill."

He taps some keys and says, "Bail is five hundred dollars. I'll need ID," he says when he sees me pull my checkbook out of my purse. I hand him the check and my driver's license. He enters the information and picks up the phone. "Athena, bail for McNeill is paid."

He hangs up and says, "She'll be out shortly. Have a seat," he says, pointing at a row of chairs. I take a seat and text Damien.

Me: I'm bringing Mel here to spend the night.

Damien: I'll get a pot of coffee brewing and make up the guest room.

Me: Thanks, love you.

Damien: Love you more.

About twenty minutes later, another officer escorts Mel out. I get up and give her a big hug. Her eyes are red and puffy. She doesn't say a word as we walk out, so I say nothing either. Once we're in the car, I look over at her. "You're coming home with me tonight."

"Thanks. I'm so sorry, Lex."

"For what?"

"Waking you."

"Don't be silly. I'm your best friend and I'm always here for you. What happened?"

"I punched Trish, and she called the cops."

"I'm sure she deserved it. What did she do?"

"Can we wait until we get home to talk?"

"Of course."

An awkward silence fills the car for the rest of the ride. We pull into the garage and head inside. Damien pours us each a cup of coffee, gives Mel a comforting squeeze on her shoulder. He takes the dogs upstairs so she and I can talk.

"You know you found a keeper," Mel says.

"Sure do. Now, sweetie, tell me what happened," I say.

Mel takes a deep breath. "I was at mom's for my step-dad's birthday. Trish, of course, was being her usual charming self."

"Of course."

"Trish asked me for money yet again and I turned her down. My mom started getting on my case about it. My Aunt Betty defended me, and that was all it took for the bitch to fly off the handle."

"What did she say?"

"She brought up all the stuff from when my dad passed. Before I even knew what I was doing, my fist connected with her nose. She called the cops, and they arrested me."

"Oh, sweetie, I'm so sorry. That punch was well-deserved if you ask me."

"It really was. And can I tell you a really terrible secret?"

"Of course."

"It felt damn good," she said with a small laugh.

"That's my girl," I say and give her a big hug. "In all seriousness, I know everything your dad put you through. Despite that, you still did more than he deserved. Why can't Trish see that?"

"Because then she can't play the martyr. It's the only way anyone pays attention to her. She only asked me for money because my Uncle Allen was talking to me about how successful I was at my job. They're the only ones in my family that are proud of me."

"I remember them and how sweet they were."

"They still are. Aunt Betty told Trish she needed to grow up and get another job if she needs money."

"Oh, she must have loved hearing that."

"I just don't get why her and my mom think I'm obligated to take care of her."

"I don't either."

"I just wish I didn't have to do this alone."

"You have me."

"I know, Lex, but I mean having someone like you have Damien. And before you say it, that doesn't mean the cowboy."

"But, Mel, he-"

"No. End of story."

I nod, not wanting to upset her after what she's been through tonight, but we will revisit this subject down the road. Mel lets out a loud yawn. I put our empty mugs in the sink and turn off the coffee maker.

"Come on. I have something you can sleep in."

"Thanks. For everything, not just tonight."

"Always!"

I grab a t-shirt and shorts for Mel, hug her goodnight and close the door to the guest room behind me. I crawl into bed, smiling as Damien pulls me tight against him. Thinking about everything Mel's family has put her through over the years, my eyes spill over, dampening Damien's arms.

"What's wrong?" he whispers in my ear.

"I just want Mel to be happy. I want her to find what we did."

"I know. Just remember, it has to happen naturally. Or we send Dave in again," he jokes.

I laugh and give him a light kiss. Feeling Damien's warm body against mine and listening to the light snoring from the dogs, I close my eyes, knowing just how blessed I am. The next morning, I wake up alone. I look at my phone and can't believe it's almost ten. I throw my robe on and walk down the hall to check on Mel, but she's nowhere to be found. The clothes I lent her are folded on the bed. I can't help but wonder how she got home. I decide I'll head to her house later and check on her. When I get downstairs. Damien's sitting at the kitchen table in just his boxers, always a sight to behold.

"Good morning, my sexy sleepyhead," Damien says.

Walking over to him, I stand between his legs, lean over, and kiss him. His hands squeeze my ass as he deepens the kiss. He pulls me onto his lap as his tongue explores my mouth. Out of nowhere, my stomach growls, causing Damien to break the kiss.

"Looks like I have two hungers I need to satisfy, baby."

"Mmmm, yes, my sexy husband."

"I'll probably regret asking, but what do you want for breakfast?"

"Cereal works."

"You don't want me to cook?"

"Oh, I do, but not in the kitchen."

"Damn, Fuckzilla!"

Chapter Ten

Damien

"Naked, now, woman!" Lexi quickly removes her clothes. I'll never tire of seeing that woman in all her naked glory. I yank my boxers off, freeing my already hard cock. After scooping my sexy wife into my arms, I walk over to the bed and lay her down. I join her and pull her in close. Crushing my lips to hers, I leave her with no doubt of my desire. She tugs at my hair with desperation.

"Fuck, I want you," she purrs. "Please, let me taste that cock."

"Get that hot mouth around my dick now," I command.

She gets on all fours and takes my entire length down her throat. She slides her lips and tongue up and down my shaft as a growl rumbles from deep in my core. I slide a couple of fingers inside her pussy as I tease her clit with my thumb. She moans hard, the vibration sending sensations down my cock. She gently massages my balls with her hand while she gives me one hell of a blow job.

"Fuck, woman," I groan as I feel my balls tighten. "I'm coming," I shout as I fill her mouth. I watch her swallow me down.

She licks her lips and moans, "Tastes so good."

"On your back, woman, and spread those sexy legs wide."

She obeys and I respond, "Good girl. Do you want your reward?" She nods. "Then tell me what you want."

"I want to feel your tongue in my pussy. Please, baby, I crave you," she begs.

I slide up her body and crush my lips to hers. She moans into my mouth as her nails rake down my back. I move down and suck on her neck, determined to leave my mark on her. That earns me a slap on the ass and I suck her neck harder. She writhes against me, desperately trying to stimulate her pussy.

"Lie still, baby, or no more pleasure."

I run my tongue down the front of her neck and between her breasts. I suck them one at a time, flicking her hard nipples with my tongue. "Please, Damien, I can't take much more. My pussy needs you now."

Without responding, I continue the sweet torture, showering her stomach with kisses and love bites. I skip the place she most wants me to and go to work on the insides of her thighs. Her moans become more desperate. After I've sucked my way up and down the inside of each thigh, I finally give her what she wants.

I slowly swipe my tongue between her folds and lightly lick her clit. Her hips buck as I increase the pressure on her clit, while I slide a couple of fingers inside her. Fuck, she's so wet for me. I suck her clit hard while my fingers stroke her g-spot. She unleashes a stream of every swear in existence, then makes up a few new ones. Her body convulses as she explodes around my fingers, soaking them as she squirts.

"FUCK! DAMIEN! SO FUCKING GOOD."

"Damn, you're the hottest woman on earth. Get ready for more pleasure."

A bright smile fills her face. I go to our "Dirty Drawer" and grab our box of KY Yours and Mine. I grab the purple bottle, squeeze some onto my fingers, and cover her pussy. She grabs the blue bottle, squeezes the lube in her hand and strokes my shaft until I'm covered. I lay on my back and look at her.

"Get that hot pussy on my dick. Now!"

She straddles me and grabs my dick, guiding it to her pussy. She slowly slides herself down until my entire length's inside her. Damn, this woman is heaven. She writhes around my dick and fuck, it's the most incredible thing I've ever felt. She sits up straight, my dick still buried deep inside her, an image I'll never tire of seeing. She leans back, using my thighs to brace herself, and slides her soaking wet pussy up and down my dick.

It doesn't take long for her to have me on the brink of explosion. My breathing shallows and my groans get louder. She slows down her pace, each trip, and down my cock agonizingly slow. I can barely remember my name as she fucks me. She moans louder as she nears her own orgasm. She enters turbo mode and fucks me harder and faster than ever before until we're coming together, both of us screaming until our throats are sore.

* * *

"Get that sexy butt moving woman," I yell.

"I'm ready."

My jaw drops when I see Lexi in her low-cut Eagles shirt. They should have her on the sidelines to distract the other team with those sexy breasts. "Forget the party. We're going back to bed," I tease.

Her smile lights up the room. "Just you wait until we get home, especially if my Eagles win!"

"Damn, woman!"

We load the dogs in the car and drive to Helen's. She agreed to watch all the dogs so we could party. We pull into her driveway right after Dean and Alex. The four of us walk in together, along with Maggie, Dave, and Holly. We're just getting ready to head out when Mikael and Hannah arrive to drop off Leo and Cocoa. We all thank Helen and head to the club.

"Lex, did you leave any Eagles merch for anyone else?" Dean teases.

"Nope," Lexi says, a huge smile on her face. "I've loved this team since I was a kid and I've been waiting a long time for this."

"Seriously, girl, it looks amazing," Hannah says.

"I'm so glad you're all here tonight. I need to go check in with Cassie and the team. The VIP table is ours, so take a seat."

I walk over to the bar with Lexi. She gathers the staff in the kitchen for a quick meeting. "Thank you all for being willing to work tonight. We completely sold out tonight, so we'll be packed. My plan is to have last call at the end of the third quarter so you can all watch the last quarter," she tells the staff.

"We appreciate that," Cassie says, "but we'll lose money that way. I've already talked to the staff, and we were thinking we stop about halfway through the fourth."

"Wow, thank you for taking that initiative. I appreciate it. Is there anything anyone needs before we start?"

Nobody had anything, so Lexi and I joined our friends at our table. I noticed there were still two empty seats. I feel Lexi nudge my side and nod towards the door. Mel and Judd are walking in together.

"Hmmm," Lexi whispers.

"Could just be a coincidence," I say.

"Sure," she smiles.

Nobody says anything other than hello when Judd and Mel sit down. We're all convinced something's going on there, but we're respecting that they've not said anything. I know it's slowly killing Lexi, but she's been behaving.

"Now that we're all here, what does everyone want to drink?" Lexi asks.

The group consensus is beer, so Lexi gets up to head to the bar. "I'll go with you," Mel says.

I lean over to Judd and whisper, "You two look good together."

"We're not together. I was pulling into the lot at the same time as her," Judd says.

The look on his face when Mel returns with a tray of glasses says otherwise.

Chapter Eleven

Lexi

"Holy shit. Holy shit. Holy shit," I scream as the last seconds tick off the clock.

"The Philadelphia Eagles are your new Super Bowl champions," Terry Bradshaw's voice booms out from the club's massive speaker system.

Damien grabs me and twirls me around. I look around the club, grinning from ear to ear as I watch everyone hugging, giving high-fives, screaming, and doing celebratory dances. The club clears out quickly, with people eager to join the party in the streets of our small town. I lock up the club and we all join the party, which goes until well after the sun comes up. After a couple hours of sleep, Damien and I head back to the club to finish cleaning up.

"So, I said something to Judd when you and Mel went to grab the beer," Damien says.

"Oh yeah? What?"

"I told him he and Mel looked good together."

"And he said?"

"He insisted they weren't together. That they just got to the parking lot at the same time."

"Uh huh, not sure I believe that."

"Yeah, same. I watched him when Mel got back with the glasses and he's definitely into her. Maybe literally."

"Why, Damien, I'm shocked at such naughty thoughts," I joke.

"Right, Fuckzilla, right," he teases.

I'm about to respond when he grabs me and crushes his lips to mine. Throwing my arms around him, I return the kiss, our tongues dancing passionately. I jump when I hear a loud round of applause.

"What're you all doin' here?" I ask our friends.

"We came to help clean up," Alex answers. "And more than just each other's mouths, like you two were doing," she teases.

With everyone's help, it only takes us about an hour to get everything done. Our friends head home and I walk up to my office to get a deposit ready. Damien takes a seat on the couch in my office while I count all the drawers and put the deposit together. Once I have everything in the bank pouch, I shut down my laptop and join Damien on the couch.

"Now that you're done, how about I leave you a deposit," Damien says.

"And just what are you planning to deposit and where?" I say.

"Get that sexy little ass naked and find out!"

"Yes, sir."

"Ooh, I like that. Good girl."

I never thought it would, but fuck, it turns me on when he calls me a good girl. I clear off my desk, and once I'm naked, I sit and spread my legs wide. Damien doesn't move from the couch. He sits and stares at my naked pussy, which turns me on even more.

"See something you like?"

"Hell yeah. Now, let me see you touch it."

I start feeling self-conscious. I've done this before, so what the hell? "I can't," I whisper.

"Why not?"

"I'm just not attractive enough," I say as my eyes threaten to spill over and I hang my head.

Damien gets up and walks over to me. He puts his hand under my chin and lifts my head. "You, baby, are the sexiest, most beautiful woman I've ever known. Always hold that beautiful head up high."

A smile replaces my tears. I hate I still have these moments of self-doubt. But I can always count on Damien to make me feel better. He scoops me into his arms and carries me to the couch. After laying me down, I watch him undress, licking my lips as he reveals more and more of his sexy body.

He lies on top of me and as he's kissing me, I feel him slide inside me. HIs thrusts are slow and gentle. The angle of our bodies allows his dick to stroke my clit with every thrust, and I quickly come undone. His breathing shallows as he increases his pace. He growls as I feel him empty inside me. He positions himself behind me, wrapping his arms around me.

"I love you, baby," he whispers in my ear.

"I love you so much," I respond. "I'm sorry about earlier."

"Sorry for what?"

"Acting stupid."

"Listen to me. It's okay to have those doubts sometimes. Your parents put you through hell."

"But not when it messes up what we're doing."

"You were just on that couch with me. Did anything feel messed up?"

"No, but the desk, what you asked me to do."

"I never want you to feel uncomfortable. Besides, and never tell anyone, but I love the sweet, slow lovemaking even more than the hard, fast fucks."

"Really?"

"Mmmm, the slower we go, the more I get to savor your incredible body. Nothing feels better than being inside you, loving you."

"Oh, Damien."

We lay together, holding each other, until I hear a noise downstairs. "Shit, the staff is starting to arrive."

We quickly dress. I grab a brush out of my drawer so I can straighten my hair. After grabbing the deposit, I lock the office and we head downstairs. Cassie's standing behind the bar and the look she flashes tells me she knows what happened in my office.

"I was just getting the deposit ready," I say.

"So that's what the kids are calling it these days," Cassie teases.

Feeling the heat rise in my cheeks, I swat Damien's arm when he laughs. We head out so we can get to the bank before it closes.

"How about pizza?" I ask Damien once we're back in the car.

"Sounds perfect."

I grab my cell and put the order in, as Damien heads toward the restaurant. He picks up dinner while I wait in the car. I smile when I see a six pack of beer and a six pack of wine coolers for me. We put the pizza out of reach of our two furry chowhounds and head upstairs to get in our jammies.

"What do ya wanna watch?" Damien asks.

"Cobra Kai!"

"Again?"

"Hey, Johnny Lawrence is sexy as hell!"

"Excuse me? What about me?"

"You're hot, but can you do karate?" I tease.

"Wax on, wax off," Damien jokes.

"I wanna see you wax off."

"My naughty wife!"

We cuddle under a blanket while we watch Cobra Kai. Again! I love being in Damien's arms, though. My favorite is when we're naked. We end up binging the entire season one before heading off to bed.

* * *

"Baby, wake up," I hear Damien say. "We need to shower and get dressed."

"But it's early."

"I have a surprise for you, but you need to get that sexy little butt up and ready."

After we shower, we head back to the bedroom. Damien hands me my Eagles jersey and hat. No way! We can't be? Can we? I can barely contain my excitement. We head downstairs to feed the dogs. I hear a knock at the door.

"Hey, Judd," Damien says. "Thanks for dog-sitting."

"Of course. Have fun," Judd says. Damien helps him get the dogs into his truck. Just after Judd backs out of our driveway, a party bus pulls in.

Chapter Twelve

Damien

I open the door to the bus and Lexi squeals when she sees our friends dressed in Eagles clothes.

"Oh, my god! Are we really heading to Broad Street?" Lexi exclaims.

"Damn right, baby. No way I could let you miss this moment," Damien says. "Mel sends her regrets, but she couldn't get the day off from work."

"I wish she was going, but I have to admit, I don't think anything could dampen my spirit today," Lexi says. "I can't believe I get to watch the Eagles Super Bowl parade in person!"

Lizzie's boss got us reserved spots in the press area, so we'll have a perfect viewing spot plus VIP parking. We pull up and there's already a sea of green-clad fans waiting. I look over at Lexi and she's bouncing in her seat like a kid on Christmas morning.

"I know I said this already, but I can't believe I get to experience this," Lexi squeals.

The driver pulls us into the parking garage for the press and we only have a short walk to the bleachers set up for us. Lizzie's boss meets us and hands us each a lanyard with a press pass inside. Lexi practically flies over to the bleachers, the smile refusing to leave her face.

I turn my head when I hear horns and see the lead vehicle carrying the Super Bowl trophy. I grab my phone so I can take some pictures for Lexi. Of course, my first one is of my beautiful wife screaming for her team. As truck after truck goes by, filled with the players and their families, the crowd cheers. The atmosphere is awesome and I smile witnessing Lexi experience this moment.

"I have an enormous surprise for everyone," Lizzie says when the last truck has gone by. "Lexi, you may want to sit down," she teases.

I grab Lexi as Lizzie fills us in.

"We're attending a reception for the team at the Linc," Lizzie says.

Lexi's jaw drops, but no sounds come out. She's quiet for the walk back to the party bus. We all pile into the bus and she still hasn't spoken.

"Earth to Sexy Lexi," I tease.

"This day can't be happening. This has to be a dream," Lexi says.

"I'm happy to pinch you," I tease.

That earns me a swat on the arm as everyone laughs. When we arrive at the stadium, we're taken to the VIP entrance to wait for the team. A man approaches our group while we're waiting.

"Hey, Scott," Lizzie says. "Let me introduce you to everyone. Of course, you already know Andy. Going around the circle, Dean, Alex, Mikael, Hannah, Johnny, Eden, Damien, and our superfan, Lexi."

Scott shakes everyone's hands. "Nice to meet everyone," he says. He's met with a chorus of nice to meet you, too.

"Thank you so much for this," Lexi says.

"My pleasure," Scott says, just as cheers erupt.

A team official carries the Super Bowl trophy into the room and places it on a table behind a roped area. The official grabs a microphone and addresses the crowd. "For anyone who wishes, please lineup for a turn to have your photo taken with the trophy."

Scott turns to the group and says, "It's supposed to be one picture per person, but I got the okay for each couple to get a picture, then one group picture for all of you."

We take our place in line and after we each get our couple's picture done, Scott waves us all over so we can line up on either side of the trophy. Lizzie hands her business card to the photographer so he can email our group's pictures. Lexi motions me away from the group.

"Thank you so much for today," she says, still smiling.

"You're welcome, but Lizzie is the one you should be thanking."

"Well, I certainly will, but in the same way, I plan to thank you later," she whispers.

"Hey, that could be hot."

"Damien!" she laughs.

I hear louder cheers and see the players file into the room. We rejoin the group and watch as the players make the rounds. When Lexi's favorite player, Jason Kelce, walks over to us, I grab her.

"I see you're wearing my jersey," Jason says to Lexi. "I'd love to sign it for you."

She nods, but says nothing. Jason smiles and turns to me. "Thank you, Mr. Kelce," I reply. "She'd love it."

"Jason, please." He turns back to Lexi. "What's your name?"

"Lexi," she answers, giggling.

"Well, thank you for all the support," Jason says as he signs her jersey.

"Would you mind taking a photo with me and my husband?" she asks.

"I'd love to."

"Hey, Dean," I call out. When he walks over, I hand my cell to him. Dean snaps the picture. Jason shakes my hand and gives Lexi a hug before he heads over to another fan wearing his jersey. We get to meet several more players before the reception ends. Heading back to the party bus to begin the journey home. We make plans to meet for dinner at our favorite pizza place.

After we get dropped off, we drive over to Judd's house to pick up the dogs. "I didn't think you'd be back this soon," he says.

"I hope we didn't interrupt anything," Damien says.

"Not at all."

"Thanks again for watching them. We're all meeting for dinner tonight. Care to join us?" Damien says.

"Appreciate the offer, but I have plans," Judd says.

"Well, enjoy and thanks again for watching the furries," Damien says.

"Any time."

"Okay, woman, what's that look?" I ask when I see Lexi's raised eyebrows.

"I swear I could smell Mel's favorite perfume."

"Hmmm, and Judd has plans. Interesting, no?"

"Very interesting," Lexi says as she grabs her cell and dials. She puts the phone on speaker.

"Hello," I hear Mel say.

"Hey, girl, wish you could've been with us."

"Me too, but work couldn't wait."

"I get it. So, I called to see if you wanted to join the group for dinner tonight."

"Thanks, but I can't. I already have dinner plans."

"Well, have fun. I'll see you in the morning. What time do I need to pick you up?"

"I have to be there at 9."

"Okay, I'll be there at 8:30."

"Thanks for taking me."

"You got it."

"Bye, Lexi."

"Later, Mel."

"Well, that certainly makes things even more interesting," Lexi says.

"It sure does. Are you sure you're okay going by yourself with Mel?"

"Of course. We shouldn't be long once they call her. Her lawyer thinks she'll just get a warning since it's her first offense and it's just a misdemeanor."

"I'm sure. If you change your mind, I'm happy to drive."

"Thanks, baby."

After we get home from dinner, we're barely in the front door and Lexi's all over me. We race upstairs and she spends the rest of the night thanking me for today.

Chapter Thirteen

Lexi

"I'm going to see if Mel wants to grab lunch after her hearing," I tell Damien while we're finishing breakfast.

"Sounds good," Damien answers as we hear a knock at the door. I see Judd standing on the other side when I answer.

"Hey, Judd," I say.

"Howdy. You look nice," Judd says.

"Thank you."

"I came to talk to Damien."

"He's in the kitchen. I need to run, so feel free to join him."

"Thanks."

"I'm heading out," I call to Damien.

"Okay. Hey, man," I hear Damien say.

I put Octane on my car radio and hear a familiar voice. I can't believe they're still playing the song I recorded in Dean's studio. The traffic light turns red, so I grab my phone and snap a picture of my name on the screen. I pull into Mel's driveway and she's waiting outside.

"Thank you for coming with me," she says.

"I'd never let you do this alone," I reply.

"But you're still a newlywed."

"What did I tell you before the wedding? I was yours first."

"Well, I still appreciate it."

"Any time. After we're done, I'm taking you to lunch so we can relax."

"That sounds perfect. Promise me we'll never stop having 'just us' time."

"I promise!"

We get to the courthouse and I pull into the parking garage. We get inside and go through security. I see a man approaching us.

"Good morning, Melissa," he says.

"Good morning, Wesley," Mel says. Turning to me, she says, "Lexi, this is my lawyer Wesley Evers. Wesley, my best friend, Lexi St. James."

"A pleasure ma'am," Wesley says.

"Nice to meet you," I say.

"We need to talk strategy before the hearing," he says to Mel.

"Which way do I head for the courtroom?" I ask.

Wesley points me in the right direction, then takes Mel to talk. I walk down and take a seat. A few minutes later, I feel a presence next to me and look up. "What are you two doing here?" I ask.

"We're here to support Mel," Damien says, nodding toward Judd.

"Thanks, guys."

I see Mel and Wesley come in and take a seat in the section designated for defendants. Promptly at 9AM, the bailiff walks to the front of the courtroom and says, "All rise. The honorable Harry T. Stone presiding."

Judge Stone takes his seat on the bench and instructs everyone to sit. There's a few cases ahead of Mel's, and it's a little after eleven when Judge Stone calls her name. Mel and Wesley walk up front.

"Miss McNeill, it says here you punched Trisha McNeill after an argument in her home. How do you plead?"

I hear a snort and look over. Trish is sitting there, a smug look on her face that makes me want to slap her silly. I take a deep breath and feel some of the anger dissipate. Mel looks at Wesley, who nods. "I plead guilty, your honor," Mel says.

"As this is your first offense, and no weapons were involved, I'm letting you go with a warning. As you paid your bail in full, no additional fines were due. You're free to go."

"Thank you, your honor," Wesley responds.

"This is bullshit!" Trish stands and yells out.

Banging his gavel, Judge Stone shouts, "Order in the courtroom!"

"That bitch left me with a bruise. She's a worthless loser who deserves to be in jail," Trish shouts.

"Young lady, one more outburst and I will find you in contempt," Judge Stone says.

Ignoring the judge's order, Trish continues, "Fuck you, Mel."

"I'm holding you in contempt of court. Bailiff, please take this woman into custody," Judge Stone instructs.

"Yes, your honor.."

We watch as the bailiff handcuffs Trish, reads her rights, and removes her from the courtroom. Judd, Damien, and I walk out and wait for Mel. She and Wesley join us a little while later.

"Thanks, Wes."

"My pleasure. Take care of yourself. Oh, and for the record, I completely understand why you did what you did."

Mel smiles and turns to us. "Thanks for being here."

I can't help but notice Mel fixes her eyes on Judd when she says that.

"Would you ladies mind us crashing lunch?" Damien asks.

"That's up to Mel," I say.

"I'd love for you to join us," Mel says, her eyes still focused on the sexy cowboy, whose face lights up when she speaks.

We walk to the parking garage together and I see Judd's truck next to my car.

"Mel, would you like to ride with me, so the newlyweds can ride together?" Judd teases.

"I don't know. If we leave them alone, they may not make it to lunch," Mel laughs.

"Hey!" I say.

"Well, she's not wrong. There's always that possibility," Damien piles on.

I toss my keys to Damien while Judd opens his truck door and helps Mel climb in.

"Follow my lead," Damien says once we're in my car. He leans over and puts his hand on the back of my head. I lean in and he crushes his lips to mine. I throw my arms around his neck as the kiss deepens. Even though we're just teasing Mel and Judd, my sexy husband's kiss is getting me hot. For a minute, I think we actually may miss lunch. My stomach has other ideas and growls audibly.

Damien breaks the kiss and says, "I better get you fed."

"Then later, you can feed my other hunger."

"Stop that, or I'll be waiting in the car while you eat lunch."

All I can think about now is Damien with a hard-on, and I feel familiar wet heat between my legs. Fuck, I want this man. Judd and Mel are already inside when we arrive at Angelo's. We join them at the table. Damien and Judd each order a beer, while Mel and I order a glass of Moscato. Damien also orders pizza and garlic knots for the table.

When our drinks arrive, I raise my glass. "To Mel, who finally got a slight chance to witness karma at its finest."

We all clink glasses and take a sip. A little while later, our food arrives. The whole time we're eating, I see Judd and Mel stealing glances at each other, convincing me more than ever that something's going on. I keep quiet, which nearly kills me. Judd offers to drive Mel home, so we hug goodbye. As we're driving home, Damien says, "If those two aren't fuckin'."

"I know. I kept seeing the looks they gave each other. It's killing me not knowing."

"I'm proud of you for being such a good girl."

Holy shit! My core throbs with desire at hearing him say that. "Please, drive faster," I beg.

"Why so eager, babe?"

"I can't take another minute without your dick inside me."

Damien makes it home at record speed.

Chapter Fourteen

Damien

"King's full. Read 'em and weep, boys," I say. I'm about to pull the chips my way when I hear a voice.

"Not so fast, my man," Judd says.

My eyes go wide when he shows his hand. "Four aces! Damn dude," I say.

"Sorry, man," Judd says.

"No worries, great hand," I say.

"So, what's everyone got planned for our gorgeous ladies for Valentine's Day?" Dean asks. "Alex wants to go to Baltimore, so we're headed there."

"I'm taking Hannah to her cabin for a naughty weekend," Mikael says.

"Eden said she wanted to stay in, so I'm cooking her a romantic dinner," Johnny says.

"I'm taking Lizzie to Atlantic City. I rented a fancy suite at the Hard Rock," Andy says.

"I'm taking Lexi to Pocono Palace Resort," I say. I hear a chair slide and see Judd walk out of the room.

"Shit," Dean says. "I keep forgetting he and Mel aren't actually together."

"At least, as far as we know," I add.

We get outside just as Judd's truck is backing out of my driveway. "I'll smooth things over tomorrow. Don't sweat it guys," I say.

We decide to call it a night, so the guys all head home to wait for our wives to get back. I'm sitting on the couch, still pissed at myself, when Lexi gets home. The smile on her face fades when she sees me.

"What happened?" she asks as she sits next to me.

"What'cha mean?" I ask.

"The look on your face when I walked in."

"We fucked up tonight."

"Tell me what happened."

"We had just finished a hand of poker when Dean asked everyone's plans for Valentine's Day."

"Oh no. In front of Judd?"

"Yeah. He got up and left without a word. I feel like such a dick."

"You aren't. We've talked so much about our theory of him and Mel. It's easy to forget we don't know if they're actually together."

"I'm going to talk to him tomorrow."

"I'm sure he knows nobody meant to upset him."

"I hope. So, tell me, how was your night?"

"We had a blast. We went to the bar you and I saw Mel and Judd at. We did a group karaoke number and a lot of dancing."

"I'm glad. You ladies deserve the best."

"Thanks. And, hey, speaking of Valentine's Day, what was your answer?"

"You said you didn't want anything special, so I didn't plan anything," I fib.

"Okay," Lexi says and walks upstairs.

I'm gonna pay for that tonight but that'll make my surprise even better. After I put the dogs out, I lock up and join her upstairs. She gives me a quick peck on the cheek, then turns her back toward me without a word. I smile, knowing I'll more than make up for it. It's just going to be a long couple of days.

The next morning, while Lexi's down at the club doing payroll, I take the dogs outside and see Judd.

"Hey, man," I yell. "Got a minute?"

Judd walks to the fence so I walk out there, the dogs hot on my heels.

"What's up?" Judd asks.

"I wanted to apologize for last night. We didn't mean to be so insensitive."

"It's okay. I'm happy for you all that you've found that someone."

"What about you?"

"No more mentions of me and Mel. It's never going to happen. I've told you before, she deserves better."

"Got it. I gotta run. I still need to make arrangements for the dogs."

"I'm happy to watch them."

"Are you sure? I was an ass last night."

"You weren't. I love having those two here. Makes it less lonely."

"Thanks, man."

"You got it."

Judd goes back to work, so I call the dogs and wait for Lexi to get home. When I hear her car pull into the driveway, I stand on the other side of the door waiting for her. She brushes right past me with barely a look. Thank god Valentine's Day is tomorrow. The next morning, Cassie calls to help me put my plan in action.

"I gotta run. Cassie just called and said something happened at the club," Lexi says.

As soon as she pulls out of the driveway, I grab the bags I packed and text the driver I hired. I run the dogs over to Judd's and see the limo just pulling in when I get back. The driver pulls up in front of the club. The driver opens my door so I can get Lexi. I see Cassie at the bar with Lexi.

"What are you doing here?" she asks when I walk over to the bar.

"Just seeing if you need help," I say.

"There's inventory missing," Lexi sighs.

"Oh no, what's missing?" I ask. I glance at Cassie, who's trying not to smile.

"Some of our top shelf vodka," Lexi says.

I glance at the papers she's holding and say, "I think you're looking at the wrong page."

Lexi turns the page and when she reads the "inventory note," she looks up at me, a smile forming on her face.

"You can breathe now, Cassie. Thanks for your help with this," I say. "Now, are you ready, Mrs. St. James?"

"I am, Mr. St. James."

"Give Cassie your car keys. Mel will be by later to take it home for you," I say.

Lexi grabs her keys from her purse and hands them to Cassie. We head out to the waiting limo. Once we're inside, the driver closes the door and we're off to paradise.

"Where are we headed?" Lexi asks.

"You'll find out when we get there. And by the way, I fibbed a bit the other night. I planned this trip months ago."

"I'm sorry for the way I've been acting. I shouldn't have been so bitchy."

"You weren't. I just wanted this to be an extra-special surprise, since it's not only our first Valentine's Day as husband and wife, but it's also our first Valentine's Day period."

"I love you, and I can't wait to see where we're going."

"I love you."

I wrap my arm around Lexi and she lays her head on my shoulder. We stay like this until the limo pulls to a stop. Lexi lowers her window and squeals, "Pocono Palace!"

Our driver opens the door and helps Lexi out. I climb out and wait for him to get our bags. A bellhop meets us and loads up our bags. We follow him inside so I can check in. After we have our room key, the bellhop takes us to The Roman Tower Suite. Lexi gasps when we walk inside.

Chapter Fifteen

Lexi

I'm completely speechless when I walk inside. A beautiful living room is on the lower level. The carpet and sofa are a matching red. The wall across from the sofa features a large, wall-mounted TV and a fireplace. After the bellhop leaves, we walk upstairs. If possible, it's even more stunning than the living room. Rose petals are sprinkled throughout the suite.

The bedroom features a round, king-sized bed and a second large TV. There's also a seven-foot tall champagne tower hot tub, a heart-shaped heated swimming pool, and a massage table with a heat lamp. We go back downstairs and Damien shows me the special gift he got for us.

A large gift basket sits on the living room table. When I look inside, I see a log for the fireplace, bubble bath, candles, a box of chocolates, a silver champagne bucket, a bottle of Verdi champagne, champagne glasses, and two robes. I keep spinning around, trying to take it all in.

"Okay, wifey, spill it."

"Spill what?"

"How many places have you pictured us having sex?"

"You'll find out," I tease. "Will we be going out to eat tonight?"

"No way, woman, I don't intend to have you in any clothes other than that robe. I've arranged for our meals to be delivered. Tomorrow night, though, I have a special surprise in store."

"I can't wait."

Damien turns on some music and holds out his hand. I put my hand in his and he pulls me close. Our bodies sway to the romantic beat.

"Happy Valentine's Day, my love," Damien whispers in my ear.

"Happy Valentine's Day, baby," I purr.

"Being here, with my wife in my arms, is the happiest I've ever been."

"Oh, Damien. I never thought this was how my life would turn out. I'm so thankful Dave knocked me on my ass. But right now, I think I want to test out the sturdiness of the bed," I say, as I head towards the stairs, with my sexy husband hot on my heels.

"Come on, let's get in bed," I beg when we're upstairs.

"In due time, my love. Right now, I want to pamper you. Strip for me and lie face down on the massage table," he says. "I'll be right back."

I put my hair up in a messy bun and lie down. Damien returns to the room, carrying one of our bags. He pulls a familiar-looking bottle out of the bag.

"Baby, get ready for a slow, sensual massage first with my hands then with my tongue."

"Mmm, Damien," I say as my body shivers at the mere thought of what he's got planned.

The delicious scent of pineapple fills the room. Damien starts at my ankles and massages each of my calves. He works his way up to the backs of my thighs, then moves to my naked bottom. I notice he spends an extra long time rubbing my ass.

"Feels so good," I moan.

"This is only the tip of the iceberg, baby."

I feel massage oil dripping onto my back. Damien's strong hands caress my back and shoulders, and I feel like I'm floating on a cloud. His lips find my neck. He sucks hard and the sweet sting only adds to my excitement at what's coming. He runs his tongue down my spine and I shudder as goosebumps appear on my skin.

My moans increase when I feel him showering my bottom with kisses, followed by some very naughty love bites. He spreads my legs slightly and his tongue finds the insides of my thighs. He grabs a towel and wipes me down.

"On your back. Now!"

I turn over and Damien picks me up. He carries me to the bed and lays me down.

"You look stunning surrounded by rose petals, my beautiful valentine. Please let me take a picture."

"Okay. But only if you promise you'll never show anyone."

"Of course not. This is for me and me only. Now, give me your sexiest look."

I see Damien's jaw drop and I'm not sure if that's good or bad. I get my answer when I look at his pants. He snaps a couple of pictures and puts his phone down. He quickly removes his clothes, his dick standing at full attention. I can't help but smile that it's me who has that effect on him.

"Stunning," he whispers before his lips crash into mine. I open for him and feel his tongue exploring my mouth. He runs his hands up and down my body as we kiss. After that incredible massage on the back of my body, he turns his focus to the front. He alternates between licking and nibbling at my neck.

Damien grabs my arms and puts them above my head. "So beautiful," he moans.

He runs his hands down my underarms and along my sides. I giggle at how much that tickles. My giggles turn to moans when his mouth goes to work on my breasts. He sucks them hard, leaving some very naughty hickeys behind. As his tongue trails down my stomach, my desire is almost too much to bear. I ache to feel his tongue between my legs and I writhe against him.

He slides down my body and tickles my feet. His hands slide back up my legs and spread them wide. A grin fills his face as he stares at my pussy. That only serves to excite me more. I can't take even one more second of this.

"Oh god, Damien, please, baby, please touch my pussy."

"My, my, aren't we eager?"

"I want you so damn bad," I beg.

My words flip a switch and before I realize what's happening, Damien's tongue parts my folds with a slow swipe. His mouth covers my pussy as he alternates between slow licks and hard sucking. The combination of sensations makes me feel like I'm levitating.

"Ahhh, it feels so good. Mmmm, baby," I moan. I lose all track of time thanks to Damien and his magical mouth. He sucks my clit hard as I feel his fingers slide inside me with ease. I quickly explode around his hand, my body bucking off the bed. My body quakes as he keeps sucking. Each orgasm comes faster and is more intense until I'm hoarse from screaming.

I push him onto his back and get on all fours. After licking his pre-cum, I open wide and slide my mouth down onto his rock-hard dick. I bob my head fast, stopping to swirl my tongue around the head. Fuck, he tastes so good. I move my head down, gently sucking one ball at a time. A growl forms in his belly, sounding like a bear's in the room.

"Oh, fuck, woman. So good, babe."

"Mmm, please, I need to taste you and swallow you."

With a deep growl, Damien fills my mouth with his salty goodness. I swallow him down, clean his dick with my tongue, and lick my lips. His dick gets hard again as he watches me, so I straddle him, taking every inch of him inside me. He pulls me down against his chest.

He grabs onto my ass and slides my body up and down his cock. My fingers get tangled in his hair. I try to sit up, but he wraps his arms around me and holds me tight.

"Baby, I want this to last. I want to savor every single second that I'm inside you."

"Oh, Damien," are the only words I can remember at this moment.

He rolls us over and begins slowly sliding in and out of me. I love every position we've ever done, but missionary is secretly my favorite. The intimacy of being able to gaze into those beautiful sapphire eyes is heavenly. I wrap my arms around his back, feeling his muscles flex with every sweet thrust. I can tell he's close when his thrusts come harder and faster.

"Oh, god, I love you," he groans as I feel him empty inside me. He rolls onto his back and wags his finger at me. I climb back on top. His dick's still hard enough to caress the magical parts inside me. I sit up and ride him hard and fast until I see colors as my body quivers around him.

"I love you, Damien," I cry out as I ride waves of pure ecstasy. I flop down next to him. We lay there for a long time, a tangled mess of sweaty body parts, chests heaving, completely spent from mind-blowing sex.

Chapter Sixteen

Damien

"Baby, wake up," I say, gently nudging my sexy wife. She slowly opens her eyes and stretches out her arms. Neither of us has budged since we finished making love. Naked naps with this amazing woman are one of my favorite things. I caress her cheek as I lay a soft kiss on her pretty mouth.

"I'm starving after that workout," she says, a sleepy smile appearing on her face.

"Me too. Let's grab a quick shower, then head downstairs to order."

"Now, why would I want to take a hot, steamy shower with you?" she teases.

"Hey! Is that anyway to talk to the man who just rocked your world?"

"My, my, you sure think highly of yourself!"

"You know you want me, Fuckzilla!"

"Meh," she says, shrugging her shoulders.

Feigning shock, I stand up, pick her up off the bed, and carry her over my shoulder to the bathroom. I open the door of the glass shower stall and set her down inside. Joining her, I turn the water on, steam quickly filling the stall. She grabs the bottle of men's shower gel and squeezes some into her hands.

I close my eyes as I feel her soft hands washing me. Her touch excites me like nothing else and my dick responds. She grabs my dick and quickly gets me off before she finishes cleaning my body. I rinse off, then grab her bottle of shower gel. My hands caress every inch of her silky skin. Slipping my fingers inside her, I return the favor, holding her as she comes. After we dry off, we put our robes on and head downstairs to order dinner. All I can think about is my sexy wife, completely naked under that robe.

"How about a fire?" I ask.

"Oh yeah," she purrs.

That's my Fuckzilla. I get the log that came with our goodie basket and get the fire started while we wait for our food. The look on her face lets me know this is going to be a passionate night. I hear a knock on the door about half an hour later. A silver cart is sitting outside with several food domes. I wheel the cart into the living room.

"That smells delicious," she says.

"Nothing but the best for my woman."

Lexi sets out the plates in front of the fire while I grab the champagne and glasses. We sit down in front of the fire. I look over at Lexi and the top of her robe opens just enough. All I can do is sit and stare.

"Excuse me. My eyes are up here," she teases.

"I wanna bury my head between those fun-bags."

"Oh, I think you'll get that chance. But first, Fuckzilla needs food."

That strikes me, and I start belly-laughing. "Life with you is never dull."

"You ain't seen nothin' yet, baby."

I pour two glasses of champagne and hand her one. "To us."

We clink glasses and each take a sip before devouring the most divine filet mignon and lobster tail I've ever tasted. After we finish eating, we share a sinful chocolate lava cake. I load the empty dishes onto the cart and return to Lexi. I pull her tight against me, laying her down as I claim her mouth.

Lexi opens her robe, exposing her naked body and my dick responds with vigor. I feel her hands tugging at my robe. She opens it and slides it off of me. She wraps a hand around my dick and pumps me. I press my naked skin against hers as she moans into my mouth. She wiggles out of her robe and pulls me down against her.

Spreading her legs, she says, "Please, baby, make love to me."

I grab my dick and slide inside her. The heat of the fire warms my naked ass, but not nearly as much as this heavenly woman sets my body and soul ablaze. Wrapped in a loving embrace, we sensually move as one. The only sounds are the crackling of the fireplace and the moans of two people who love each other more than life. When we finish, we lay together in front of the fire, enjoying more delicious champagne.

"Thank you for the best Valentine's Day ever," Lexi murmurs through a yawn.

"Sounds like someone played too hard," I tease.

"Because of my horny husband, whose dick is always hard."

"Excuse me, Fuckzilla? You're way hornier than me!"

"Liar, liar, pants on fire. Oh, wait, you're not wearing pants."

Without another word, I stand up, pick my naughty wife up and toss her over my shoulder. She swats my ass the entire way up the stairs. I take her into the glass-enclosed swimming pool stall and unceremoniously deposit her in the water.

"What the hell was that for?"

"You needed to cool off," I say as I join her.

"You're in trouble now, hubs."

Before I can respond, a wave of water hits my face. Oh, so that's what we're doing now. I splash her back. She splashes me even harder, then takes off. I chase her, but every time I catch her, she breaks free. Our naughty game continues until we're both out of breath. Lexi throws her arms around my neck. I pull her tight and kiss her hard, leaving her no doubt how much I want her.

"Baby, I need to fuck you right here, right now," I say.

"Oh, Damien, please. I want you."

I pick her up, my hands holding her sexy little ass. "Wrap your legs around me, baby."

She locks her legs around my waist.

"Good girl. Now, grab my dick and get it inside that sexy pussy."

"Mmmm," she moans as I feel first her hand, then her pussy around my cock.

"Keep those legs locked tight and get ready to ride." Holding her waist, I bounce her up and down on my dick, the heated pool water splashing around us. Damn, she feels incredible. Her sexy breasts bounce against my chest, just adding to my pleasure.

"Oh, fuck, Damien, I'm so close. Please, harder, oh god, oh Damien," she cries out as her body quakes in my hands. Her dirty mouth sends me over the edge and I fill her. I lift her off my sated dick and after a few cool down laps around the pool, we grab a quick shower and head to bed.

Chapter Seventeen

Lexi

S tretching as my much-needed slumber ends, my nose fills with the smell of bacon and coffee. Bacon is my favorite meat. Okay, my second favorite, I laugh to myself. After a day of indulging in my favorite meat, I'm famished. I look at the end of the bed and see my robe. I get up and wrap my naked skin in its soft material, then head downstairs.

My heart skips a beat when I see my sexy husband sitting on the couch. A new food cart sits in the living room. The mix of sweet and savory smells causes my stomach to rumble. Damien looks at me, a smile appearing on his face as he says, "Let me guess, Fuckzilla needs food."

Laughing, I reply, "Oh yeah, thanks to you."

Damien picks up the gold carafe sitting on the cart and pours two cups of coffee. I smell my favorite creamer flavor, hazelnut, fills the air as I prepare my cup. Damien fills two plates with a pile of cheesy scrambled eggs, crispy bacon, and cheesy shredded potatoes.

"Everything smells so good. I don't know what to eat first," I say.

"I have a suggestion," he says, pointing at his lap.

"Horndog," I tease as I savor a mouthful of the most delicious scrambled eggs I've ever tasted.

"I need to keep my Fuckzilla satisfied."

"Oh, baby, you definitely do!"

"I hope you're ready for another action-packed day."

"I can't wait to see what you have planned."

"You'll find out soon enough, but first, after we finish breakfast, how about a dip in the champagne glass?"

"Sounds perfect."

We head upstairs, remove our robes and get into the whirlpool. The champagne glass shaped structure sits seven feet tall and features relaxing jets. A sense of sleepy calm washes over me as I let my eyes fall closed. I could sit here all day.

"I think we need one of these at home," I say, only half-jokingly.

"I'd never get you out of there," he says.

"Just bring me wine, chocolate, and dirty romance novels, and I'd be good."

Smiling, he says, "I love you."

"I love you too."

We're downstairs cuddling on the couch when I hear a knock on the door of our suite.

"I'll get it," Damien announces as he rises. "Thank you," he says and closes the door.

I watch him walk back to the couch, two garment bags in one hand and a shopping bag in the other. Curiosity gets the best of me.

"Does this mean I get to find out my surprise?" I beg.

"Not yet, and don't you dare let me catch you peeking."

I jut my lower lip out and Damien laughs. "You look cute when you pout, but that won't make me give in, woman."

"Fine," I say, crossing my arms across my chest. Another laugh from Damien.

"We need to get ready. Join me in the shower."

I practically fly up the steps, watching from the top as Damien carries his surprises upstairs. After a long, luxurious shower, I'm standing in the bathroom, one towel around my body and one around my hair, when I hear another knock. Damien puts his robe on and walks downstairs. He returns with two women wearing smocks.

"Babe, Nina and Jackie are here to help you get ready," Damien says. He disappears into the bedroom and closes the door.

"Mrs. St. James, please have a seat at the vanity," Nina says.

I smile at the sound of my married name. Nina and Jackie stand behind me, examining my hair.

"I think a Dutch braid is perfect," Jackie says.

"I agree," Nina says.

Jackie gets to work on the braid while Nina opens her makeup kit. "You have the most stunning green eyes," Nina says.

"Thank you."

Too embarrassed to look in the mirror, I focus my gaze on the floor the whole time Nina and Jackie work on me.

"Stunning," Jackie says.

"I agree. What do you think?" Nina asks.

I don't answer, still unsure I want to see myself.

"Sweetie, you really need to lift that pretty head. You're gorgeous, and that man is lucky to have you."

I finally lift my head and I can't believe the woman looking back at me. "You two must be magicians," I say.

"No, honey, we're artists and we do our best work on a beautiful canvas like you. Now, let's get you dressed," Nina says.

Jackie unzips my garment bag and my eyes go wide when I see what's inside. I can't believe he remembered. One of my all-time favorite romance movies is Pretty Woman, especially the scene where Edward takes Vivian to San Francisco. I sit, mouth hanging open, gazing at an exact replica of the red gown Julia Roberts wore in that scene.

Jackie hands me a small bag and I pull out matching red lace panties and bra. They step out until I have the lingerie on, then help me with the dress. I sit down and slip the matching red dress flats onto my feet, loving Damien for remembering how much I despise heels. I finish the look with the long white dress gloves.

"Are you ready to knock that man's socks off?" Nina asks.

Smiling, I respond, "Yes. Thank you so much for everything."

"Our pleasure," Jackie says. "Wait here until we introduce you."

I hear Jackie and Nina descend to the living room.

"Mr. St. James, please allow us to present your beautiful wife," Nina says.

I walk to the stairs, pausing at the top so I can memorize Damien's face. His jaw drops and he's rendered speechless. I carefully make my descent, loving the hunger in his eyes. As I approach him, I notice he has one hand behind his back. Expecting to see a bouquet of flowers, I'm instead presented with a large red velvet box.

It's my turn for a jaw drop when Damien opens the pretty box. I stare at the most beautiful ruby earrings and necklace I've ever seen. "Happy Valentine's Day, again, my love."

"Oh my, Damien, they're stunning."

"Like the woman who's about to wear them. They're not as high value as the set in the movie, but also unlike the movie, these aren't on loan."

I smile, completely stunned that I'm the owner of such beautiful jewelry. I put the earrings on, then Damien takes care of the necklace. The light touch of his fingers sends chills down my spine. I smile even wider when I finally focus my attention on Damien. He's sporting a stunning black tuxedo, the tie and cummerbund the same shade of red as my dress.

"Would one of you mind taking a few photos?" Damien asks the ladies.

Nina takes his phone and snaps a few pictures of us, standing arms linked, huge smiles plastered on our faces. Nina hands Damien his phone. He takes an envelope out of the pocket inside his jacket and hands it to Nina. "Thank you both."

Damien hands me a Christian Louboutin red clutch handbag. We finish our outfits with cashmere dress coats. Walking outside, Damien leads me to a waiting limo. The driver stands by the back door, opening it when we approach.

"Good evening, sir. Please help yourself to the complimentary champagne."

Once we're in the limo, the driver closes the door and exits the parking area. A short time later, after downing two glasses each of champagne, we pull to a stop at the VIP entrance of the Mohegan Sun Pocono casino. Arms linked, we walk to the High Roller area. We're greeted and led to a private poker room. I can't believe my eyes when I see who's sitting around the table.

Chapter Eighteen

Damien

"I'm guessing you recognize everyone," I say.

"Oh my god, yes. Starting closest to me and going clockwise, that's Phil Hellmuth, Antonio Esfandiari, Patrik Antonius, Paul Wasicka, Phil Laak, and Tom Dwan," I answer.

"Impressive, love," I say.

"How did you know they would be playing here tonight?"

"I may have arranged it."

"Wait... what? Why? And how did you know who my top favorites are?"

"A little bird told me."

"A little bird named Mel, perhaps?"

"I'll never tell."

"So, who else is coming?" Lexi asks.

"Nobody."

"But there's two empty seats with chips stacked."

I watch Lexi's face when Phil Hellmuth, her all-time favorite player, stands and walks over to us.

"We've heard you're quite the player. Please, join us," Phil says.

Lexi stands, frozen in place for a moment. I walk over to her and take her hand. I walk her to the empty seat between Phil Hellmuth and Antonio Esfandiari, her other favorite. The rest of the players stand until Lexi's seated. I walk to the other empty seat and we all sit. A dealer comes in and we start our game.

I'm the first one eliminated, but damn, my wife is holding her own. She pushes all in against Phil Laak. The board shows the queen of diamonds, two of hearts, seven of spades, and nine of clubs. The dealer deals the river and I see the queen of spades. His chip count is lower than hers, so she can eliminate him with the right cards.

"Call," Laak says, pushing his stack to the middle. He flips over two kings, a smug look on his face. Lexi looks down and I think she's had, but then she flips her cards. My eyes go wide when I see the queen of hearts and the queen of clubs. Holy shit, my baby just knocked out a poker pro.

Phil stands and walks over to Lexi. He shakes her hand before walking over to sit with me. One by one, the rest of the players are eliminated until only Lexi and Phil Hellmuth remain. I'm truly in awe of this amazing woman. Lexi has a slight edge in her chip count. She's small blind in this hand and Phil is big blind.

Lexi looks at her whole cards and raises pre-flop. She either has something good or she's trying to bluff a legend.

After studying her for a few minutes, Phil calls. The dealer deals the flop. Queen of hearts, ten of hearts, and two of clubs. Lexi bets and Phil calls. The turn gives us the seven of spades. Lexi and Phil both check. The river. King of hearts. Lexi shoves all in. She has Phil covered so she can't be eliminated, but a win for him leaves her with very little. Phil snap-calls and turns over his cards. The eight and six of hearts. Fuck. A flush. That hand will be tough for Lexi to beat.

A huge grin fills her face as she turns her cards over. I jump out of my seat and run over to her when I see the Ace and Jack of hearts. The room erupts when everyone realizes Phil's flush just got beat by a royal flush, the best hand in poker. And that hand belongs to my wife!

"Damn, woman," I say as I pick her up and twirl her around. "Do you realize what you just did?"

Her eyes go to her feet and her smile fades. "I'm sorry," she whispers.

"I didn't mean it that way. You just beat six poker pros. AT POKER!"

Her smile returns as the players approach her, each of them shaking her hand and congratulating her. The dealer snaps pictures of all of us. A casino employee joins us, handing a wood box to Lexi. She opens it, and inside are all the chips that were used tonight. Since they were special collectors' chips, they have no monetary value, but for Lexi, they'll always be a reminder of what she did tonight. The players all sign the felt inside the box.

"We'd be honored if you and your husband would join us at Ruth's Chris Steakhouse for dinner," Phil Hellmuth says to Lexi.

She glances at me and I nod. "We'd love to," Lexi says.

Two golf carts wait outside the VIP room to take us to the restaurant. We laugh and talk throughout dinner. Phil endured some good-natured ribbing for losing to Lexi. Watching her so comfortably interact with some of her idols, I think back to that woman who wouldn't even look at me that first night in the club.

It's well after midnight before we're in the limo, heading back to our suite. Lexi lays her head on my shoulder and falls asleep, not waking until the car comes to a stop. The driver helps her out and I follow. I pay him and we head inside. Apparently her catnap in the limo gave her a second wind and Fuckzilla emerges.

"Please, Damien, take me to bed and fuck my damn brains out."

We race up the stairs and all I can think about is getting her out of that dress. I stand behind her and tug at the zipper on her dress as she slips out of her shoes. The dress pools at her feet and all I can do is stare at my wife standing there in the sexiest red lingerie I've ever seen. The cheeky panties I picked out show off just enough of her sexy, round ass. And hot damn, her cleavage spilling out of her bra is almost more than I can handle. "Baby, you look so hot that my dick could double as a hammer right now."

Lexi saunters over to the bed and lies down. My heart threatens to beat right out of my chest. Not to mention there's about to be a hole in the front of my pants. She grabs her phone and a minute later I hear the opening notes of Right Said Fred's 'I'm Too Sexy.' If she thinks for one second that I'm stripping to this song...

"Strip for me," she commands. "And I better enjoy it or you don't get this," she says, running her hands down her body.

And that's all it takes. A command from my sexy lover and I'm stripping to this damn song. I hate this song, by the way. But fuck that red lingerie. I give her an ass shake and I'm met with claps and giggles. I love the sound of her laughter, so I channel my inner goofball and unleash the silliest struts and dance moves I can fathom. My clothes are off by mid-song, but I keep dancing for her, dick fully erect, until the song ends.

"That was a definite ten, my love. Now, get your ass on this bed and make me scream."

Chapter Nineteen

Lexi

"Baby, you look like you just got off a horse," Damien teases.

"Spending hours riding dick'll do that to a girl," I fire back. I slowly make my way to the bathroom. My soreness is a pleasant reminder of the mind-blowing night Damien and I had when we got back to the suite.

"So, I can claim victory? Fuckzilla was finally defeated?"

"You will henceforth be known as Hammerdick after that pounding you gave me."

That earns me a smack on my ass as he follows me to the bathroom. We share one final steamy shower in this amazing suite. We dress, then pack our bags. I'm attempting to make the bed; a hard task since sheets and blankets are everywhere. Did I mention last night was mind-blowing?

Damien walks up behind me and wraps his muscular arms around me. "I think you need to wear a braid more often," he says.

"Oh, is that so?" I tease. A heat spreads between my legs when I remember being on all fours. Feeling him pull on the braid while fucking my pussy from behind was beyond hot.

"So fucking sexy," he whispers in my ear. My body shivers in response.

We're just reaching the bottom of the stairs when I hear a knock. One last silver cart filled with delicious food. The room fills with the scent of vanilla and cinnamon. We indulge ourselves with French toast and more hazelnut flavored coffee. The limo arrives around eleven to take us home.

"Thank you for this incredible weekend. My first Valentine's Day celebration ever was beyond my wildest dreams," I say.

"Your first with me, you mean?"

"Uh, no, first ever. Nobody ever cared enough. Then amazing you comes along and gives me a weekend I will never forget. I love you so much," I say, linking my arm through Damien's and laying my head on his broad shoulder.

"I hate that's how you were treated, but I'm honored I got to be your first. I'm crazy in love with you."

"First and only, my love."

When the limo pulls into our driveway, we climb out. The driver hands us our bags. Damien pays him and we head inside. After we drop our bags in the living room, we ride over to Judd's house to pick up Maggie and Dave. Damien knocks and my jaw drops when the door opens. I look over at my husband and he has the same look on his face.

"You're home early," Mel says, her face turning a dozen shades of red. "I just stopped by to check on the dogs. I look down and notice she has no shoes on. Interesting.

"Who's at the - oh, hey guys. Welcome home," Judd says. He's also barefoot and, if I'm not mistaken, his hair looks a bit tousled.

It's taking every ounce of self-control not to squeal and ask a million questions, but the last thing I would ever do is embarrass our friends. But, oh my god, do I want to know what's been going on. I can't be mad at Mel for holding out on me. But damn, if she ever admits it, she better give me every detail, especially size!

Damien recovers first and says, "Thank you again for taking care of the dogs."

Hearing their daddy's voice, two balls of fur come rushing to the door. They both sit. I see Dave look back and forth between Judd and Mel, and I'd swear on my life he was trying to tell me something. This is one of those times that I wish dogs could talk. Mel hurries off and returns with the dogs' stuff.

Taking the bags from her, I smile and say, "We need to chat soon." Mel flashes me an uncomfortable look. "I have a lot of details to tell you."

Mel sighs and says, "I'll call you."

"Can't wait," I say with a wink.

As we're walking back to the car, I hear Judd's front door close. We get the dogs loaded up and head back to our house.

"Holy shit," I exclaim.

"My thoughts exactly," Damien says. "Did you see his hair?"

"Yep, that and they were both barefoot. Our friends are doin' the deed,' I joke.

"Bumpin' uglies," Damien says, laughing.

"Wait, wait, wait, I have the perfect one. Knockin' da boots," I say, before I snort-laugh so loud, Maggie and Dave bark.

"I mean, Big and Rich tell women to ride a cowboy," Damien says.

By the time we're parked in our garage, we both have tears streaming down our faces and our stomachs are killing us. I sit down on the couch and a fresh round of tears flows.

"Are you okay, sweetheart?" Damien asks.

"If they really are together, I'm so happy for them. I love that girl so much and I want her to be happy."

"I wanna see Judd with the same thing. We just need to give them space."

"I promise I'll behave."

"That's my good girl," Damien says.

"Uh oh."

"What?"

"You've awakened Fuckzilla."

"Hammerdick to the rescue," he says, pulling me into his lap.

One glorious hour later, we slide the couch back to where it was and head upstairs to shower. We're back on the couch watching TV when my cell rings.

"Maybe it's Mel," Damien says.

"I'm betting she's otherwise occupied at the moment." I look at my phone. "Hey, Cassie."

"I hate to bother you at home, but we have a problem," Cassie says. I put the phone on speaker.

"What's going on?"

"Manny just quit. He got a job at the new casino that just opened."

"I'm on my way," Damien says.

"Thanks, guys. See you soon," Cassie says, and disconnects.

"Guess that makes up my mind about cooking at the club, at least for now," Damien says.

"Not how I planned it to happen! Let me grab my coat," I say.

"No, you stay here with the dogs. I got this."

"You sure?"

"Yeah. I'll call if I need anything."

After Damien's gone, I get the dogs their dinner. While they eat, I make myself a grilled cheese sandwich and a bowl of tomato soup. After we're done, I bundle up and take the dogs for a quick walk. Of course, they both do their business in McDickhead's yard. I quickly clean it up before he catches us and we head back home.

I do some tidying up around the house, then sit down to watch a bunch of reruns of Friends. When I tire of watching Ross pine for Rachel, I switch TV for music and decide to catch up on some reading. My two favorite indie authors both had recent releases. I have the paperbacks on my shelf but haven't read them yet.

"Which one should I read first?" I ask Maggie and Dave. They both tilt their heads at the sound of my voice, but offer no input. "Well, you two are a big help," I laugh. The hell with it. I grab both books and return to the couch. Holding one book in each hand, I alternate between each book, one chapter at a time.

"That's a sickness, you know," Damien teases.

I was so wrapped up in the books, I never heard him come in. "I can't help that Lala Montgomery released 'Operation I Do?' only a week after JJ Grice released 'Burn It Down.' I couldn't pick which to read first, so here we are! Both books are amazing, just as I knew they would be! Now, tell me, how'd it go?"

I put a bookmark in each book and lay them on the coffee table and wait for Damien to join me.

Chapter Twenty

Damien

"I had a blast. And I'm definitely inspired. I want to expand the menu."

"With you cooking full-time?"

"No. I enjoy it, sure, but I don't wanna give up my nights with you."

"So, what are you thinkin'?"

"I'll cook until we find someone."

"Sounds perfect. I'll get an ad up on Indeed tomorrow. I'll also call Eden and see if she knows anyone looking."

"Cool. Thanks, babe," I say, failing to stifle my yawn.

"You sound exhausted. Let's go to bed," Lexi says.

"I wanna grab a quick shower first. The grill made me feel greasy.

"I'll put the dogs out while you shower, then I'll be up."

I hear a wolf whistle as I walk upstairs. After getting undressed, I get in the bathroom before my favorite nympho comes upstairs. I take my boxers in the bathroom with me. By the time I get done, Lexi's in bed, sound asleep, surrounded by our fur-kids. I move Dave so I can get in bed, give my wife a quick kiss on the forehead, and turn off the light.

I have the bed to myself the next morning. Jeez, even the dogs didn't stay with me! When I get downstairs, I understand why. A plate of cooked bacon sits at the back of the counter. Two furry butts are sitting on the floor in front of the counter, tails wagging. Lexi's standing next to them.

Her robe is hanging open, revealing her sexy tank top and boy shorts, her hair piled in a messy bun on top of her head. She's sipping a cup of coffee and if it's the sexiest damn thing I've seen. Well, not as sexy as the red lace lingerie, but there's just something about this look that drives me wild.

"Breakfast, honey?" she says.

I walk over and pull her tight. "Yes, dear," I tease.

Lexi breaks some eggs in the skillet and throws some shredded cheese in. I love her cheesy scrambled eggs. I stand behind her, arms around her, nuzzling her sexy neck.

"Okay, Hammerdick, I'm trying to make you something to eat."

"I'm already holding what I want to eat."

She turns her head around and gives me the dreaded eye roll. I refuse to let go while she keeps cooking. "If you don't quit poking me in the ass..." she teases.

"Not my fault. You look so damn sexy. Hammerdick is powerless against your feminine wiles."

She somehow finishes cooking with me draped all over her. After breakfast, we head upstairs. She strips and sits down on the bed, leaning back against her pillow. She spreads her legs wide and, never breaking eye contact with me, says, "I believe I heard you say you wanted to eat me. Well, what're you waiting for?"

I quickly pull my clothes off and crawl across the bed. Wanting to taste her so badly, I don't wait. I bury my head between her sexy thighs while I work my magic on that sweet pussy. Fuck, she's so damn delicious. I lick and suck her hard, quickly making her scream as her orgasm overtakes her body. She trembles as I replace my tongue with my dick. We fuck hard and fast, and it doesn't take me long to fill her with my cum.

After we're showered and dressed, we drive down to the club. I sit with Lexi at her desk while we post the ad for a new cook.

"So, I was thinkin' about something," I say.

"I can only imagine," she teases.

"Not that. I was thinkin' of maybe tryin' some different food items to see what sells."

"I like that idea."

"So you approve?"

"Of course, but you don't need my approval."

"But this is your club."

"No. It's our club."

"I was thinkin' for tonight of adding crab cakes and maybe a meatball parm sandwich. If things don't sell well, I won't add them permanently."

"Mmmm, they both sound delicious. I'm done with the ad, so let's head to the store and grab what we need."

"Thanks for supporting this," I say.

"You're an amazing cook!"

We walk downstairs and Cassie's at the bar. The timing couldn't be better. "Babe, would you mind going to the store so I can bring Cassie up to date?" I ask.

"Not a problem. Just need your keys," Lexi answers.

"So, what did you need to go over?" Cassie asks.

"Some changes to the menu."

Lexi smiles and waves. As soon as she's outside, I say, "Okay, that was a cover. One sec." I dial Mel's number.

"Hello," Mel says.

"Hey, I'm here with Cassie. Let me put you on speaker. I wanted to talk to you both about a surprise party for Lexi's birthday."

"I'm excited already," Mel says.

"What did you have in mind?" Cassie asks.

"I wanna do it here. The first part could be before the club opens with just our friends and the staff, then continue when we open with a special karaoke night," I say.

"I have a great idea to get her there," Mel says. "I'll need your help Cassie."

"Sure, what are ya thinkin'?" Cassie asks.

"I'll invite her for lunch, telling her that since Damien gets to celebrate her at night, I get lunch. Then you can call her and tell her there's a problem at the club."

"That's perfect," I say. "Cassie and Mel, can you work out the details and just let me know? That way I don't get caught. I really want to surprise her."

"Sorry to interrupt, but Lexi just pulled into the parking lot," Scott yells from the DJ booth.

"Mel, I'll call you later," Cassie says and we disconnect.

"Real quick, before she gets in, the plan is to try out different menu items, see what sells and what doesn't. Tonight is meatball parm sandwiches and crab cakes," I say.

"Got it," Cassie says with a wink.

Not even a minute later, Lexi walks in with two bags of groceries.

"Anything else in the car?" I ask.

"Nope, all set. Now, I wanna watch my man in action," Lexi says.

"Not in front of the staff," I tease.

"Honestly, Hammerdick," she sighs.

Cassie's jaw drops. "What did you just call him?" she asks.

"Hammerdick," Lexi says, smiling.

"Yeah, well, she's Fuckzilla," I say, pointing at my wife.

Laughing, Cassie says, "Oh my god, you two are hilarious."

Lexi follows me into the kitchen and unpacks the bags. "I wanna be your sous chef."

"So, I get to order you around?"

"Mmmm, yeah," she purrs, earning an eye roll from Cassie.

Lexi gets the crab cake mixture ready. I pull out enough to make one and have her put the rest in the fridge. Grabbing a skillet, I lightly coat it with olive oil and heat it up. Once the pan is ready, I cook up the crab cake. When it's done, Lexi and Cassie each try a bite.

"Oh, baby, tastes so good," Lexi moans.

"Honestly, woman," I tease.

"This is delicious," Cassie says. "I think this'll be a hit tonight."

I get the meatball mixture ready. Lexi and Cassie both offer to help make them, so I show them what size I want.

"I love holding your meaty balls," Lexi jokes.

Cassie laughs so hard, tears stream down her cheeks. "These are even better than Schweddy Balls," she adds.

"Not you too," I joke. "I thought you were both ladies."

"Hell, no, hubby," Lexi says.

"I view that as an insult," Cassie jokes.

I listen to the two of them trade increasingly dirty food innuendos while I make my sauce. "Now I know what they mean by food porn," I joke.

Once we get everything ready, I put the meatballs in the oven, then add them to the sauce when they're done. I carry the large pot to the fridge.

"I need to get you home, so I can come back here to prep everything else," I say to Lexi.

"Okay. Later, Cass. I had fun," Lexi says.

"Me too."

"Be back soon," I say and take Lexi home to the dogs.

Within a week of placing the ad, and with Eden's help, we have our new cook. As much fun as I was having, I'm grateful to be back home with my woman every night. I love preparing meals for my gorgeous wife, but my preferred place to cook will always be the bedroom!

Chapter Twenty-One

Lexi

I'm awakened the morning of my birthday to 'Birthday' by The Beatles. I stretch and sit up. Damien's standing at the foot of the bed. I look down and lose it. He's completely naked, except for the bright pink wrapping paper sticking out from his pelvic region.

"Happy Birthday, baby," he says, as he gyrates his hips. "Wanna unwrap your present?"

"Mmmm, yes please, sexy."

The wrapping paper makes a crinkling noise as he crawls across the bed. He lies on his back and I can't help but laugh at the bright pink paper sticking up in the air. I shimmy out of my pajamas, then crawl over to him. Starting at the base of his dick, I slowly slide the paper off, stroking his cock as I go.

"Since it's your birthday, you get to do anything you want with me," he says.

"I wanna ride that sexy cock, baby."

"Fuck, woman."

I climb on top of my sexy gift and grab his dick. I slide my pussy until he's all the way inside me.

"Fuck, you feel so damn good inside my pussy."

I lean back, feeling pressure on my clit and my g-spot. Damien runs his hands up my stomach and gently massages my breasts, teasing my nipples with his strong fingers. He holds his hands out for me to hold. Intertwining my fingers with his, I watch his face while I fuck him. The pressure builds inside my core until I can't hold back and I soak his dick. My orgasm gushes all over him, leaving me even wetter. He pulls me down into his arms, thrusting inside me until he fills me with hot cum.

"Sit up for me, baby," he says breathlessly. "Fuck, I could stare at that hot body all damn day."

"That was the best birthday present I've ever had. I wish we could stay like this all day, but I don't think Mel would appreciate that."

"Well, then I guess we better get you showered. Let the birthday pampering continue."

"I like the sound of that."

Damien carries me into the bathroom and sets me down. He turns on the water and once it's warm, he helps me into the stall. The air fills with the scent of vanilla as he lathers my body. I sigh as his hands travel my naked skin. He rinses me off, then grabs my strawberry scented shampoo.

"I love washing your hair," he says as he tangles his fingers in my mane.

"Your fingers are magical," I sigh.

"You know it, woman!"

After he finishes with me, I get to watch Damien wash himself, which is quite the thrill. Watching those powerful hands all over the body that's brought me so much pleasure is beyond exciting. The highlight, of course, was watching him clean his dick and his sexy ass. A drop or ten of drool may have escaped my mouth.

A warm towel awaits me when I step out. He holds me tight as he dries me off. I brush and dry my hair, then removed the towel, hearing whistles and catcalls as I walked back to the bedroom. I grabbed my favorite black lace bra and panties, which I plan to have Damien remove later. Since Mel and I were going casual for lunch, I went with blue jeans, a white long-sleeved t-shirt, and my favorite black cardigan. I completed the look with my comfy black ankle boots and the ruby jewelry Damien gave me for Valentine's Day.

I applied some mascara and a light coral lipstick. Happy with my look, I smiled into the mirror. That alone is a minor miracle. I used to be horrified by the very existence of mirrors, but a certain sweet man changed all that. Walking up behind me, he put his arms around me.

"Damn, we look good together, baby," Damien says.

"We sure do. I love you."

"Mmm, love you more."

We hangout with the dogs until Mel arrives. I give Damien a kiss goodbye, then Mel and I head out to her car.

"You look amazing. Marriage definitely agrees with you," Mel says.

"Thanks! You, of course, always look amazing."

"If you say so."

"Stop! You're a hottie and you know it, girl! I bet I know at least one cowboy who would agree."

"How many times do I have to tell you? There's nothing going on between Judd and me."

I nod, but say nothing. I can't help but feel sad that my best friend feels the need to lie, but for now, I trust she has her reasons. The rest of the drive to lunch is quiet. Once we're inside, Mel orders us a bottle of my favorite wine, Moscato. She pours us each a glass.

"Happy Birthday to the best friend I could ask for," Mel says.

"Thank you," I say.

"Wanna split a ham and cheese calzone?" Mel asks.

"Sounds good."

"Hey, you okay? You seem down?"

"Nope, all good," I say and force a smile. "Calzone sounds perfect."

When our waiter comes back, Mel orders. We're just about finished eating when my cell rings. I ignore it. A couple of minutes later, it rings again.

"Sounds like someone needs you," Mel says.

"They can wait," I say.

When the phone rings a third time, Mel grabs it. "It's Cassie."

"Shit, I better make sure there's not an issue at the club."

"Hey Cass, what's up?"

"I got to the club and the security alarm was going off. The cops responded and they need you to confirm nothing was taken or damaged."

"Did you try Damien? He can also sign off."

"He wasn't picking up."

"Okay, I'll be there as soon as I can."

"Thanks."

"No problem."

I disconnect and turn to Mel. "I'm so sorry. Something set off our alarm and I need to go down there."

"No worries, we were done. I'll go pay the check and we can head out."

"Thanks."

We head out to Mel's car after she pays. "Are you sure you're okay?" Mel asks.

"I was just thinkin' about the episode of Friends where Rachel found out about Monica and Chandler."

"And that made you sad?"

"Yeah, Monica and Rachel were best friends, but Monica didn't tell her."

"Oh, I get it. Look, there's really nothing to tell."

"Okay."

Mel pulls into the club's parking lot and I see Cassie standing outside with a very handsome police officer.

"Check him out, Mel."

"Damn, he's hot."

"Yeah, and he has cuffs."

"Damn, Damien's made you naughty."

I smile as we walk over to the club.

"Thanks for coming," Cassie says.

"No problem," I say.

Cassie opens the door and I gasp when I walk inside.

"SURPRISE!"

Chapter Twenty-Two

Damien

I watch Mel give Lexi a huge hug as I walk over. "Happy birthday again, babe."

"Thank you, baby. I'm guessing you had help," Lexi says, pointing at Cassie and Mel.

"Guilty," they both answer in unison.

"And are you even a real cop?" Lexi asks the officer.

"No ma'am. Take a seat on your birthday throne," the officer says.

Lexi sits down and I signal to Scott in his DJ booth. Def Leppard's Pour Some Sugar on Me starts. I huddle with the rest of the guys at the bar while Lexi and the other girls get quite the show. After the stripper is done, Lexi walks over to me at the bar.

"So, guessing that woke up Fuckzilla," I tease.

"No way in hell. Only you can do that, Hammerdick," she says. Shit. I'm never going to hear the end of this.

"Excuse me? Did you call him Hammerdick?" Dean asks, a little louder than I would have liked.

"Now you did it," I say.

"Hey, you're the one who was so turned on by my red lace lingerie that you said your dick could double as a hammer," Lexi teases.

"Damn, red lingerie would do it for me too," Mikael teases.

Lexi saunters away as the guys tease me mercilessly. A few minutes later, I hear the women laughing and looking my way. Cassie breaks away from the pack of laughing hyenas and walks over to the bar.

"Should we get the food served?"

"Yes, thanks, Cass," I say.

After we finish dinner, I wheel a cart from the kitchen and take it to Lexi. I light the candles and lead the group in a round of Happy Birthday. Lexi blows out the candles and cuts the cake. When we're done, we all pitch in to clean up and get the club ready for our customers.

"That was part one of your celebration," I say to Lexi. "We're also having a special karaoke contest in your honor."

"Yay! Thanks so much for everything, my love," she says, throwing her arms around my neck. I pull her and kiss her.

"Get a room, Hammerdick," Dean teases, earning him a swat on the arm from Alex.

"Leave them be. They're still newlyweds," Alex scolds Dean.

Once we make sure everything's in order, Cassie opens the doors to the public. After about an hour, I walk up on the stage and grab the mike.

"Lexi, please join me," I say.

She walks up on stage and stands next to me.

"For those that don't know, my amazing wife's birthday is today. In honor of her, we're having a special karaoke contest tonight. In addition, you'll be treated to some songs by our friends. Only customers are eligible to win the contest, however. So, if you think you have what it takes, sign up at the bar. Oh, and by the way, the grand prize is five thousand dollars."

We join our friends at our table. Cassie brings us a pitcher of beer and a bottle of Moscato. We all drink a toast to Lexi's birthday and wait for the Karaoke contest to start. I see Judd lean over and whisper something to Lexi. She nods her approval, and he gets up from the table and walks onto the stage. He enters a song into the Karaoke machine and picks up the microphone.

"This one's for the woman who doesn't know she stole my heart," Judd says.

I look over at Lexi and her mouth's hanging open as she stares at Mel. Mel's face is bright red as I hear the opening notes to Kingdom Come's What Love Can Be. Judd sings, his eyes never leaving Mel's face. My sweet, sensitive wife, of course, has tears pouring down her face. I slide over and put an arm around her. She lays her head on my shoulder as we watch what appears to be the start of something very special.

"What did Mel say about Judd at lunch?" I whisper in Lexi's ear.

"She said nothing was going on between them. Either she lied to me or I'm not the only one getting a surprise tonight," Lexi whispers back.

I nudge her and nod my head towards Mel. I've seen that look on Lexi's face many times when we're making love. Mel has it bad, whether or not she knows it. Judd finishes and rejoins the table. Nobody says a word. Once all the contestants had sung, Dean and I walk up on stage.

"We will invite the top five singers back on stage to sing one more song, then all of you will vote and select our winner," I announce.

I hand the mike to Dean and he announces the top five. After everyone sings, the waitstaff hand out ballots. Once all the ballots are in, Lexi takes the box. She and Mel head up to her office to count them. When they return, she hands me the results and I go back up on stage and announce our grand prize winner. I point up to Scott.

"Now, let's see everyone out on the dance floor," Scott says.

I watch Lexi and the other girls hit the floor and damn, they look amazing. After a few fast songs, Scott slows things down, so I grab my wife. We hold each other tight as we sway to Steelheart's I'll Never Let You Go.

"Look, look, look," Lexi whispers in my ear.

I follow her eyes and see Judd ask Mel to dance. They walk out to the floor and Judd wraps his arms around her. She lays her head on his chest and wraps her arms around his neck.

"They definitely belong together," I whisper.

"I'm so happy for her," Lexi says.

"Him too," I say.

The party winds down as the night goes on. When Scott announces last call, security clears the last few patrons out.

"Do you want me to wait for you?" Mel asks Lexi.

"Thanks, but I'll ride home with Damien," Lexi says.

"I just need to drop Judd off first," I say.

"Um, I could give him a ride," Mel says.

"Thanks," Judd says. He and Mel head out.

"Oh, I bet she can give him a ride," I say.

"Damien!" Lexi says.

Once we finish cleaning everything up and the last staff members have left, Lexi and I head home. We get inside and see the dogs curled up together. We take them out for their last bathroom break.

"Babe, why don't you head upstairs? I'll be up shortly," I say.

"Don't keep me waiting. Fuckzilla is horny."

Once I hear her in our bedroom, I grab a piece of birthday cake and head up. She's already naked and in bed when I get in the room.

Chapter Twenty-Three

Lexi

"Oooh, sex and cake make Fuckzilla very happy," I say when I see Damien carrying a plate with cake on it.

He puts the plate down and gets naked. Grabbing the plate, he joins me in bed. He breaks a little piece off and feeds it to me. Swiping some icing off the top, he covers my nipples. One at a time, he licks them clean as he teases my pussy with his fingers.

He takes more icing and paints a line from my breasts down to just above my pussy. Running his tongue down my body, he cleans up every bit. He works his way down and devours me. I writhe beneath him as he sucks and licks my clit.

"Oh, Damien, that feels so good."

"Baby, you taste so damn good."

"Oh fuck," I scream as my body quakes and bucks off the bed. "Please, god, please fuck my pussy."

Damien slides up my body and lifts my ass with his hands. He slides his dick inside me with one hard thrust. I gasp at how incredible he feels. Even after all this time, I'm still in awe of how incredible sex with him is.

"Oh god, Hammerdick, pound me hard."

He thrusts into me hard and fast, bouncing my body off the bed.

"How does that feel, baby?"

"Mmm, Fuckzilla loves it. But I want it even harder." I lock my legs around him and grab his ass, pulling him even closer to me. He pounds me harder than ever before.

"Fuck, woman, I love the way my balls sound slapping against that hot ass."

"It's the hottest fuckin' thing I've ever heard. You fuck me so damn good."

"Oh, woman, nothing feels better than being inside your hot pussy. No woman has ever excited me like you. I love filling you with my cum."

"Oh, yeah, give it to me, baby. I love when I feel that warm cream flood my pussy. Fuck, I want it so bad."

I feel Damien's breathing shallow, groaning as he shoots his load deep inside me. He crushes his lips to mine, his tongue eagerly exploring my mouth. I can still feel him inside me.

"I love you so much. I never want to stop feeling like this," I say.

"I love you more than life, baby. This right here, this is heaven."

He hardens inside me. Holding me tight, he rolls over, pulling me on top of him.

"Oh, Damien."

"Baby, I wanna make love slow this time."

He keeps me tight against him and I slowly slide up and down his incredible dick, my clit rubbing his erection with every stroke. We're still going strong as the morning sun makes its appearance.

"Oh, Lexi, you're incredible," he says as he empties inside me for the fourth time. We hold each other close, our bodies drenched in sweat, sticky from icing and plenty of bodily fluids. My body tingles from head to toe. Laying here in bed with my sexy husband is bliss. As usual, my growling stomach ruins the moment.

"I need to learn to control that," I joke.

"I find it quite sexy. That performance earns you anything you want for breakfast."

"Can we go out?"

"Sounds like a plan."

Damien scoops me up and carries me to the shower. He turns the water on and pulls me close. We stand, the hot water streaming down our bodies as we hold each other and kiss. After we finish our shower, we get dressed and head down to our favorite diner.

"Thank you for easily the best birthday ever," I say.

"My pleasure, baby."

We're just finishing up when we see two familiar faces walk in and get seated in a corner booth. As much as I want nothing more than to run over and say hello, I don't want to make them uncomfortable, so Damien and I head out after he pays our check.

"I know that must've been hard," Damien says.

"It was, but the most important thing is for Mel to be happy."

I turn to look for a minute and when I see the look on Judd's face, I can't stop the tears. Mel's been through so much stuff that only I know. She deserves a man to take care of her, to love and worship her, to finally not let her down. Just like what I found with Damien. I take his hand as we walk to his car.

As we approach the official first day of spring, the weather cooperates and we get warmer temperatures than usual. We're sitting at the dog park on a beautiful afternoon. The sun is shining and there's not one cloud in the bright blue sky. As we watch Dave and Maggie play, I reach into the bag I brought and pull out a wrapped box.

"Happy Anniversary," I say.

"Um, we got married in December," Damien says.

"I know that, silly. Exactly one year ago today, a certain someone knocked me on my ass. A day that forever changed my life."

"And I couldn't be more grateful. I had no idea when I rescued that sweet boy from the shelter that he would rescue me in ways I didn't even know I needed."

"I know what you mean. That crazy girl helped me through some tough times." I hand Damien the box.

"What's this, love?"

"Open it!"

Damien opens the box, laughing when he sees what's inside. "I can't believe you had a comic book made. And you know I love the title, 'The Misadventures of Hammerdick and Fuckzilla.' Thank you."

"The inside shows the highlights of our first year together," I say.

"This is so great. And the cover is perfect," he says.

"Where else but on a bed?"

"Definitely my favorite place to spend time with you," Damien says with a wink.

"And all because of this place. I'm so glad I started coming here," I say.

"Me too. And that I found love here," Damien says.

"Looks like we're not the only ones," I say.

"What?"

I nod toward the parking lot.

"Well, well, well, would you look at that," Damien says.

We watch as the pickup truck's driver gets out and walks to the passenger side. He opens the door and helps his passenger out. They walk toward the park's entrance holding hands, wide smiles plastered on their faces. Maggie and Dave stop playing, look at each other, and emit a loud bark of approval.

"The magic of the dog park continues," I say, tears of joy streaming down my cheeks as I watch the beautiful couple headed our way.

The End

About the Author

Samantha Michaels was born in 1973 in the small town of Abington, PA and was raised and still lives in Hatboro, PA (both suburbs of Philadelphia). She is married to her high school sweetheart and they have a rescue dog, a beautiful Black Lab named Holly.

When she's not writing or working at her full-time job, she enjoys watching her Philly sports team (hopefully) win, listening to heavy metal/hard rock music, Texas Hold Em, reading, and spending time with friends and family.

Her love of reading began at a young age, thanks to her mother and Sesame Street. Her mom read to her constantly, and by three years old, she was reading on her own, and hasn't stopped. This eventually turned into a love of writing. She was writing for herself and then for a small group of friends, one of whom told her she should be writing books. She took her friends advice and has since published several romance books with plenty more on the way.

Also by
Samantha Michaels

Leather and Lace

A Second Shot at Love

Pet Shop Passion

Silent Angel

Rockin' Spring

Rockin' Summer

Rockin' Autumn